BLOOD AND RAIN

Other Books by B. L. Morgan

Blood for the Masses
Blood on Celluloid
Night Knuckles

BLOOD AND RAIN

B. L. MORGAN

SPEAKING VOLUMES, LLC

NAPLES, FLORIDA

2011

BLOOD AND RAIN

ISBN 978-1-61232-018-2

Library of Congress Control Number: 2010942889

This book is dedicated with intense love and respect to
Judi Morgan.
Without you none of this would be possible.

Special Thanks goes to Jennifer Caress for a wonderful 1st edit.
You are the real hero of the John Dark Universe.

Special dedication to Kay and Gene Ayres
Truer friends have never walked the Earth.

BOOK ONE

PART I

OPENINGS

"Mercy ain't a part of the game."
- Sonny Liston

This is when
The night crawlers
Come out . . .
- The Walker in Darkness

CHAPTER 1
WELCOME TO THE JUNGLE

There are reasons for all the things that I do. You may not understand them. Hell, I might not understand them, but there are reasons. It's Saturday night, raining lightly. I'm driving in my car, a tan Olds Delta Eighty-Eight. Just driving, watching the streaks made by the streetlights and the blinking neon lights from the taverns.

October, East St. Louis, cool, cool night, even the filtered air from the heater doesn't keep out the stink from the city around me. Whores wave, yell "Hey baby ya wanna . . .," I drive on. Feeling the heat from the blowers. Feeling the cold build inside.

I cruise the streets going nowhere in particular. Watching the show.

Then, there he is, looking big and bad and black. That motherfucker. I park and sit and watch. The drizzle comes down slow almost like a mist.

He stands there in his black leather long coat and black hat and black boots all shining in the night. Shit, he even has sunglasses on in the middle of the fucking night.

I watch from a half block away. A pair of brothers walks up to him. They exchange some words and one shows him something in his hand. The man in black leather motions them to follow him, then leads them to the dark entrance of an alley away from the streetlights, into the blackness.

People walk by the alley, young partiers going nowhere except down to the land of the wasted. Even from where I am, through the rain-streaked windshield, I see a pinprick of light flicker on, then die a moment later.

More people pass on the street. Some coming and going from a little bar called the Barbary Coast. Not all of them are lost.

A little while passes, maybe fifteen minutes, then the three emerge from the dark of the alley. They give each other *bro* handshakes.

Boy, isn't that touching. Like the spider kissing the flies.

Well, it's now or never - 11:30 in East St. Louis. There is always a reason for the things that I do.

I get out of the car. My Olds Delta Eighty-Eight, it's a classic. At least that's what the used car dealer who I bought it from said. Whatever that means.

I cross the street, weaving slightly. Kind of stumbling, hands in my overcoat pockets.

I step up onto the sidewalk, my feet dragging, and start walking toward Mr. Leatherman. They say his name is Morris West. He has a Jamaican accent. He showed up here about six months ago and has been selling crack ever since his shiny black face appeared.

Every now and then he sells some shit he says is crack and somebody dies. It's bad enough to be selling death, but to be cheating people so they die without even getting the high they paid for. Well, there ain't anything lower than that.

I stumble toward him exaggerating the drunken walk. I get close to him and say "Hey man, what you got I can get high on," Sounding as buzzed as I can.

Mr. Leatherman looks at me closely.

"I don't know you," He says. "I don't know what the fuck you talk about." He's showing his teeth like he's angry. I think *all right, show me how bad you are.*

"I got money man," I say and pull a wad of bills from my coat pocket with my left hand.

"Look man," I say, "I just want to get fucked up. I saw you here before. I know what the deal is. Look, my old lady left me, the fuckin bitch, I just need to get wasted. You're here, I got money, and you don't want to do this. I'll find somebody who'll like this money. Understand?"

He looks at me closely. "Are you a cop?" He asks.

"Ah fuck you man," I tell him, "No!"

He hesitates then says, "It would be entrapment, man, if you had any-thing to do with the police". He waves me toward the alleyway.

Mr. Leatherman, Morris West, steps back into the pitch black shadow and I follow him. He takes a pipe out of his inside pocket and from a medicine bottle puts a rock of crack into it. He flicks a Bic lighter and the flame illuminates his cold black face, his eyes like hot coals.

"Sweets to the sweet," He says and laughs deeply shoving the pipe at me.

The motherfucker thinks he's Candyman.

I pull from my right pocket a snub-nose thirty-eight with a homemade silencer on it made from washers glued together. He doesn't even seem to see me move and step close to him. I guess he thought I was going for the pipe.

I put the barrel under his chin and pull the trigger. There is a pop like a single handclap. The top of his scalp comes loose in a big flap and he steps back twice before his knees collapse. He goes down on his ass and then back in a pile of garbage.

I stand over him again and put the barrel to his forehead and pull the trigger. His head comes apart and I know the candy store on this block is going to be closed for a while.

Then, I go through his pockets and wallet and take all that he has. The cops will think this was just one more drug killing by a rival dealer and what the hell, I can use the cash.

CHAPTER 2
JACK DANIELS AND JULIA

That night I sat up and watched TV all night. Actually, I laid on the couch and drank whiskey as the images on my set just flew past my eyes. I watched old stupid horror flicks on KDNL TV 30.

Or maybe they watched me. They showed me the kind of things I wanted to see.

Death and Destruction.

That's all that's left for a man like me.

Jack Daniels didn't put me to sleep as I hoped he would.

Sunday came early, too early. Bright light through the shades. I found myself trying to close those shades and dull the razor cutting in my brain.

I guess I must have slept sometime during the night, but I didn't remember falling asleep and I sure didn't feel rested.

The sign on the door to my office/apartment reads - John Dark, Detective, Open Every Day.

Well, sometimes I just leave the door locked.

It's mainly just a front anyway. I make my real money other ways. This morning I had five thousand dollars in my pocket from someone the police will be happy to see gone.

Damn my head hurts. I pick up the JD and start to take a drink but the smell makes me wretch. I go to the bathroom and throw up. What a waste of good whiskey. The couch looks good so I fall out on it and cover my head with the pillow waiting for sleep, or at least the pounding to go away.

*   *   *

About noon or maybe about two, I managed to drag myself off the couch and make it to the bathroom. I felt like shit. The mirror told me I looked like shit. No surprise there.

I shaved, threw water on my face, and dressed in my cleanest dirty clothes - classic private eye stuff, wrinkled sport jacket and slacks.

Well, even if I do a half-assed job at this stuff, I do like the look. Every now and then I even get some pussy thrown at me because of the Mike Hammer look.

Dizzy chicks sometimes get a stoned look on their faces when I tell them what I do. And I don't have a clue as to why. I don't give a shit. I don't ask too many questions when they start feeling me up and fantasizing about Mike Hammer hammering them.

I was reaching for the doorknob to leave when the knock came from the other side.

*   *   *

She looked like the slave girl from "Gone With the Wind". The one who was always screaming and crying and yelling, "Miss Scarlet, Miss Scarlet." Except she had a calmness about herself that spoke of a life full of experience.

This is not to say that she looked like one of the prostitutes that hang out on Grand Avenue. She didn't look worn out, just weary. Aware of what the world could do to her. But not afraid of it. No, she didn't look like she was afraid of anything.

She sat across from me at my desk, the desk that came with the office/apartment when I rented it. She told me her name was Julia Richardson and that she was here because of her daughter.

"Felicia is a good girl," she said. "She makes good grades, doesn't do no drugs and runnin around and she ain't been in no trouble at all."

"That's good, I'm glad at least there's a few kids that ain't messin up. So why are you here?"

Miss Richardson looked strangely distressed like someone who wants to run but knows they have to stand and fight.

"I don't know where Felicia's at," she said, the words thick in her throat. "About three nights ago she just up and vanished from out of her bedroom."

CHAPTER 3
NOBODY SEEMS TO CARE

Julia Richardson was a small, strong built woman, dressed conservatively in a long, blue with white striped dress. She looked like a secretary for a NAACP law firm. She was a nurse.

She sat with her hands in her lap, very prim and proper. She passed me a photo of her daughter.

"The police won't do anything," she said. "They had me fill out a form and said this kind of thing happens all the time."

"I see," I said.

"No you don't," she came back. "They made it sound like she was some kind of young hoe, done run off. Hell, I know there's no sign of forced entry but that don't mean she wasn't forced."

She sounded angry and was getting hotter by the second.

"I don't know what it means," I told her.

She started to do the head-rocking thing that pissed-off black women do.

"Well, I tell you what it means," she almost yelled. "I tell ya!" Then she froze with her mouth open.

"Oh, I'm sorry," she said, "I just can't stand the way they treated me, like just some stupid nigger bitch." Tears came to her eyes. "My girl is a good girl and nobody seems to care that she's gone."

Julia Richardson stood up and turned her back on me. She wiped one hand across her eyes. She was obviously very embarrassed by her show of weakness. Black women can't afford to be weak.

I came around the desk and put my hands on her shoulders. The symbolic absurdness of a white man comforting a black woman was apparent to me. A lot of the blacks that I knew from the East St. Louis ghetto thought that whites were the cause of all their problems.

Now, she was just a woman needing some help when it looked like she could find none. And me, for a change, I was going to act like a man.

"I'll try to find out what happened to your little girl," I told her. "I can't guarantee anything, but I'll look for her."

CHAPTER 4
FELICIA

Julia Richardson gave me a recent school photo of Felicia. She was a cute kid. Soon she would be a beautiful dark woman, just like her mother. We made a list of Felicia's friends that she knew of. A short list, only two. This wasn't the type of girl who ran around much.

Julia gave me two other photos of Felicia. One with her school choir. One of her playing in a chess tournament with people watching in the background.

We made a list of Felicia's interests and activities.

She went to school, sang in the school choir, stayed overnight at her friend's houses every now and then. She was in the chess club at school. A clean innocent kid.

No boyfriend as far as her mother knew.

Sounded to me like she just wasn't out enough to have a boyfriend.

Julia Richardson was proud of her daughter. It showed on her face and in her eyes when she spoke about her good grades, how pretty she was when she was in her choir up on the stage, and how she was smart enough to beat the snotty white boys from the suburbs when her chess club went to tournaments.

Yeah, she was proud of her daughter. She was sad too. She didn't know where her little girl was. She wore her sadness like a heavy rain soaked coat.

I was tempted to tell her just how bad a detective I was. I got very few real cases and most of those were of the, follow my cheating spouse type thing. But who else could I send her to? She obviously wasn't rich and any legitimate detective agency would bleed her dry quickly.

"So," I asked Julia Richardson when it seemed like our interview was winding down. "Who told you about me?"

"When I was leaving the police department, one of the desk cops called me over and gave me your name. His name tag said Briggs and he said you know the city real well."

"Joe Briggs," I said. "Yeah, I know him. He sends me some business occasionally." I didn't tell her the business he sent me was usually a lot different than this.

"Well, I'll do what I can," I told her.

Julia Richardson stood up and we shook hands. I felt like putting my arms around her and I don't think entirely out of sympathy either.

Julia was a good looking woman. She hesitated but the moment passed. Just one more time in my life I'd missed my mark.

Then she turned and walked toward the door. She stopped and turned around.

"Oh, just one more thing," she said, "How much is this going to cost?"

"I tell you what," I said, "We'll discuss that if I find her."

Julie Richardson left then and I didn't have the heart to tell her that I didn't have any idea how to look for her little girl and I didn't expect to ever find her.

CHAPTER 5
JOHNNY'S

I put the three photos Julia Richardson had given me in my jacket pocket and went over to Johnny's Bar and Grill. I figured I could show the photos and ask around about Felicia. And it gave me an excuse to have a drink or two. Or maybe a dozen if I felt like it.

Johnny's was about a block from Dark Detective Agency, so I walked there. The city hadn't grown any prettier since I'd last seen it. Garbage was still laying in the street wherever people had decided to drop it or kick it. Drunks were standing about at the entrance to the alleys or sitting in the doorways to boarded up businesses.

If anybody walking past looked at one of the drunks too long, the drunk would give him the finger then belch or fart loudly.

The buildings were slowly collapsing. This was a dying city.

Johnny's Bar and Grill was a clean little hole in the wall where the local guy could quietly drink himself to unconsciousness without the worry of having his throat cut for whatever was in his pockets when he passed out. The main reason behind that was the guy behind the bar, Johnny Davis.

Davis was a small, black, wiry guy in his forties with a face like a piece of beef jerky. He always had a big knife in his back pocket that he could have out in a second and a half, and he always had his gun under the bar within reach.

Nothing ever happened at Johnny's Bar and Grill when he was there. And if anything did happen, he ended it real fast.

There were three people in the bar after I went in. One guy was sitting at a table mumbling to himself over his beer and the other guy at the far end of the bar was watching wrestling on a TV that was suspended from the ceiling against the back of the bar.

I walked in through the door and Johnny saw me instantly. "Oh, no," he said, "Here comes trouble, everybody out, we gotta lock the doors."

"I'll dodge the stampede," I said, "Just shut up and gimme a shot of Jack."

"Gimme died," he said, reaching for the bottle, "You don't need this. It'll make you ugly. Then again, it won't hurt you."

I downed the shot and felt the fire inch down my throat.

I took the photos out of my pocket and laid them on the bar.

"I'm looking for a girl," I say pointing to the photos.

"Little too young for you," he says, "You fucken degenerate."

"Chill out, Chuck! It's a job. I was hired by her mother to find her."

"Yeah, so who you think you are this week, Columbo or Sam Spade?"

"The way I feel today, I'd say it's Barnaby Jones. Gimme another shot."

He refilled the shot glass.

"You keep throwin gimme's at me and I'll make ya like Ironside and you can be rollin your detective ass around here."

Johnny looked closely at the photos. He had his face screwed up in a grimace like he was trying to recall a secret long buried in the deep, deep catacombs of his mind. Reminded me of one of the California Raisins.

After a long pause, he finally said, "I don't know the little girl at all, cute kid, but," he pointed at the photo where Felicia was playing chess against some white kid with several people watching in the background. "Something about this here picture just catches my eye. Like something is familiar. I don't know what though."

I picked up the other two photos and put them in my pocket. "Something familiar about that one, huh?"

"Yeah, but it probably ain't nothing. If I can figure out why it hits me that way, I'll let you know."

I picked up that photo and put it into my pocket. "Gimme another shot," I said and turned and started toward the toilet.

"What I'll give ya," Johnny said to my back, "Is a shot upside your dome with my size ten ham bone".

Before I reached the door Johnny yelled, "You gonna take a dump you leave that window open. Last time you was here the guy after you came out of there lookin like he been breathin death."

I gave Johnny the finger.

"You know where you can put that."

I went in and took my eye-watering dump. And didn't open the window. Sometimes the small victories in life are everything.

*   *   *

When I finally came out of the toilet the guy watching *Wrestling From the Chase* was gone and *Gilligan's Island* was on the TV. The other guy was still talking to his beer and Johnny was sitting at a table with a quart bottle of Jack Daniels and two shot glasses.

He was watching Ginger pout her lips at the Professor who was more interested in his test tubes, but he still heard me walking up behind him.

"If you'd stayed in there any longer," he said, "I'd have to charge you rent."

Johnny had a newspaper spread out on the table in front of him.

I asked him, "You trying to learn something in your old age?"

"Yeah," he said. "You ought a try it sometime, before your skull collapses from the vacuum in there."

Johnny pointed to a particular story.

"Check this one out," he said.

The story was a report of a man found in the alley behind a local strip club, Roxie's, with his throat cut.

"Over the last two months, I've seen five of these in the paper. Always the same. Guy with his throat cut behind a strip club, a bar or nightclub, something like that. I think we might have our own serial killer right here."

"Well," I told Johnny, "I ain't got time to be tracking no serial killer. It ain't my business."

"I'm just telling ya to watch your ass. Something is on these streets lately that ain't normal."

"I heard about Morris getting his brains blown out last night," Johnny said, "That was normal."

I was instantly alert and listening.

"He just fucked the wrong person over and he deserved what he got. But this shit," he pointed to the story again, "This ain't normal. Not for here. Not for anywhere."

I wanted to change the subject fast. I didn't want anyone around me talking about Morris West since it had been my finger on the trigger when he had departed this world.

"Say, Johnny." I said seeing that he was watching Mary Ann's ass real close on the TV, "You think the Professor ever fucked Mary Ann?"

Johnny continued watching Mary Ann, even licked his lips a couple of times. "You see," he said, "That's the difference between white men and black men. The Professor thinks it's more important to be doing that experimenting shit than he does to be laying the meat to those young healthy fillies. If I was on that show, they'd have to change the name to Fornicator's Island. I'd be fuckin MaryAnn, Ginger, and Mrs. Howell, too. You white guys think up a show and there ain't nobody fuckin nobody. That's what's wrong with the world, not enough fuckin. If everybody was fuckin all the time they wouldn't have time to be fightin all the damn time."

"I'll drink to that," I told him and we clinked glasses and downed another shot.

The door banged open and we both watched as three young black gang bangers walked in.

CHAPTER 6
LARRY, DARRYL, AND DARRYL

As the three walked directly toward the table where we sat, my hand moved instinctively to the pistol I had holstered inside my jacket.

All three wore Chicago Bull's jackets that were black with the red bull on the back. Two looked to be about sixteen, medium sized for kids that age. The other might have been nineteen. He was about six feet tall.

"Oh, shit," Johnny says to no one in particular. "Here comes Larry, Darryl, and Darryl. Better close the door."

"What the fuck you talkin about old man," the one who looks nineteen says. "You know I be Mike and this is Jamal and Terry. Who the fuck is Larry, Darryl, and Darryl?"

I tell him, "Just a joke son. Get your head out of your ass, you might see it when someone's shittin ya."

He turned to me, "Ain't no one talkin to you white boy. You just sit there and shut the fuck up! And I ain't your son, motherfucker!"

I slid my chair back from the table so I could draw faster.

Johnny spoke pointing in the young guy's face, "Slow down boy. This is my place and I'm the only one that can call that sorry piece of shit a motherfucker in here."

I looked at Johnny, "Thanks a lot buddy," I told him.

"Always trying to help ya there, John," he said.

"Yo, motherfucker," the sixteen year old called Jamal said. "We came in here to get some drink," he said drink like he was trying to clear this throat on the word.

"A lot of mothers been fucked around here," I told Johnny.

"They all were," he said. Then to the kid he says, "I done told you boys before, I ain't selling you no liquor."

The trio was getting really agitated. The two who had spoke were breathing heavy and they were trying to stare holes through both our heads. The other one who I picked as being the most dangerous was glancing around the room looking for what he could use as a weapon.

Johnny spoke again, "You young fuckheads must think you're some tough motherfuckers' right?"

The guy who had been mumbling into his beer got up and silently walked out the door. I guess he wasn't as stupid as he had been acting.

"That's right," nineteen-year-old Mike hissed through his teeth, "Ain't nobody around here as bad as us."

"Well," Johnny says, "You think you're so fuckin bad, you walk your ass back in that john back there," he motioned over his shoulder. "My man just took a shit back there and his stink will scare the hell out of anything alive. Anybody tell you that a white man's shit don't stink, my man here is living proof that they lied."

"And I didn't open the window," I said.

"Lads," Johnny says using a very fake Scottish accent, "Don't go in there. It's a fate worse than death that waits ya."

The silent sixteen-year-old Terry spoke, "Mike, these motherfuckers are crazy. We might as well leave them the fuck alone."

"I'm crazy too," Mike says cocking his head to the side trying to look deranged. "And I say when we leave these motherfuckers alone."

"Are you this crazy?" I asked Mike and slowly pulled my thirty-eight out of my holster and laid it still in my hand on the table.

All three of them stepped back and a flash of fear went across the faces of Mike and Jamal. Terry's eyes had narrowed, a small grim smile played across his lips. No fear there.

"Are ya fast Mikey?" I asked.

"Yeah," he said with a small quiver in his voice, "I be a fast motherfucker."

"Well, you're so fast," I said, "I was gonna lay it on the table and let you try to beat me to it. But hell, let's see if you're fast enough to beat me to it when it's under my hand."

I let the gun drop to the table, but kept my hand on top of it.

"Come on now," I said, "Go for it and stop me from pulling the trigger."

I could see the sweat spring up on Mike's forehead.

It was already dark outside and cool, but in here the heat was rising.

"He's bluffin," Jamal said almost whispering.

Johnny stood up slowly, his right hand out in front of him toward Mike in a halt gesture.

"Hold on man," he said, "Hold on, don't ever call this man's bluff. This man here," he nodded towards me, "Was in the Special Forces in Vietnam and he's still addicted to killing. Don't call his bluff. He can kill you in more ways than you can shake your dick. He likes it too. That's why he was a washout as a pro-boxer. He couldn't stop when he had to."

"I'm out a here," Terry said and was backing toward the door.

"You ain't goin no-where," Mike yelled at him.

"Fuck you man," Terry told him. "This ain't worth this bullshit." Terry turned and walked to the door.

"You're a punk motherfucker," Jamal said to him.

Terry gave him the finger and left.

"Looks like your troops are deserting." I said, "Now I'm getting tired of this.

When I count to three I fire."

Mike took a big step backward and put both hands in the air.

"Come on," he said to Jamal. At the door he stopped and glared at me.

"This ain't over," he snarled at me with as much menace as he could.

"You better hope it is," I snarled back.

CHAPTER 7
CHESS AND FISTS IN THE DARK

Johnny poured us another shot.

The Jack Daniels was tasting good. Fogging my brain.

Gilligan's Island went off and we watched a succession of stupid sitcom repeats. *Sanford and Son, All In The Family, Happy Days.* Laughing at some of the jokes whether they were funny or not and saying how stupid some of the others were.

We got hungry so we ordered some pizza from Dominos. Pretty sad pizza but it does fill a hole in the stomach.

The guy who delivered the pizza looked like some kind of a body builder. Big shoulders, big arms! He looked nervous as hell too. He kept glancing around the room like he expected someone to rush out of a dark corner.

People, who don't live here, don't like coming here.

So we watched TV, ate pizza and sometime during the night I talked Johnny into playing chess.

No paying customers came in, so Johnny didn't really have any excuse not to play me.

For a while he refused anyway, reminding me that it had been less than a month since I had pulled my gun on a guy who I was playing chess against.

What it was, was that the guy had thought I was a lot drunker than I was and he tried to steal one of my pieces, my Bishop, right off the board, right in front of my face, while I was looking at it. Then he told me I was lying when I told him to put the Bishop back.

So I pulled my gun and took the side bet we had. And Johnny had told me to never play chess there again.

But that was then and this is now.

I offered to let Johnny hold my gun while we played so he knew I wouldn't pull it on him.

"Naw, you better keep that gun," he told me, "Cause if I get to thinkin about how that john has got to smell since you didn't open up that window. I know I'd have to shoot ya in the foot."

So we played chess for a while and I tried my little tricks on Johnny and kept control of the board the whole time, slowly penetrating his territory and tearing holes in his defenses. After a while I was glad I hadn't given Johnny my gun cause he was pissed off.

If he wouldn't of shot me, I think he would at least shot the board.

Finally he declared, "I've had enough."

"You've been cheatin me all night," he said, "I'd kick your ass for it but I'm too tired. Guess I'll do it tomorrow."

My watch said it was a quarter to one.

Where had the night gone? So we shook hands and I told him I'd catch him later and started walking home through the misty dreary wet streets.

*   *   *

It was slick and wet and I was buzzed and wanting to get home so I could lock the door and drink some more and let the darkness take me. Maybe for the last time.

I passed the bums sitting in the doorways. I passed the black alleyways. Shuffling on. Half unconscious.

I stepped past the corner of a building near the blackness of an alley.

"Hey," a voice said in a hoarse whisper.

I turned and the fist flew out of the dark. Smashing me above the left eye. A streak of light, the force of the punch spun me. The world tilted. The ground rushed up at me.

I found myself on my hands and knees.

"Yo motherfucker," a voice said, Mike's.

I was kicked hard in the stomach. It folded me up.

"You not such a bad motherfucker now." Jamal's voice.

Another kick from the other side partially blocked with my arm.

I coughed. They laughed and tried to kick me again. Me in a ball blocking with arms and legs.

I farted.

"Oh shit," Jamal said and laughed.

I threw up into my hands, thick chunks of pizza mixed with whiskey.

"You're a sick motherfucker," Mike said and tried to kick me again.

I threw a handful of vomit in his face. He threw his hands up instinctively to wipe it off.

I caught his foot in the bend of my arm and twisted it sideways while standing to a crouch then straight armed him to the chest. He flew off his feet.

I threw a side thrust kick to Jamal's stomach from the crouch but missed. Instead I smashed his dick and balls with my foot.

He staggered back, bent at the waist, hands on balls. I grabbed his head and slammed it into my knee. Felt his nose crunch. He went down.

Mike was up and coming at me.

"Just you and me motherfucker," he said trying to bounce like Ali. But he was square to me so I knew he didn't know what the fuck he was doing.

He telegraphed a jab but was still fast enough, to catch me a glancing blow on the right side of my face.

I caught his wrist with my right hand, locked it to my neck and slightly twisted it. Then threw a hard short left upper cut to his elbow. It popped. Mike screamed and went to his knees crying like a two-year-old.

I kicked him hard in the face. He gargled from his back then rolled to his stomach and laid there moaning.

I felt in my holster. Put my hand on my gun. Not tonight, I thought. Then left them where they lay.

CHAPTER 8
JOE BRIGGS

Monday morning. The phone ringing and I float up towards consciousness like a deep sea diver when his tanks are running low.

I turn over and try to sit up. The first time I fail. My ribs on my left side
feel like they are made of broken glass. My stomach muscles don't want to
work. They feel like they've been ripped out with a garden trowel.

The phone is across the room on my desk.

I look at it from where I lay on my couch. I can barely open my left eye.
The phone looks like it's a thousand miles away. The phone rings. Sending
vibrations of pain through my head. I'd shoot the damn thing if my gun was
within reach, but it was on the floor in my holster by the door along with my
jacket, followed by a trail of shirt, shoes and pants to the couch.

The phone keeps ringing. I curse at it but it keeps ringing.

I prop myself up to a sitting position using my arms. My right arm hurts
like hell. Hell, my whole body hurts like hell.

I'm getting too old for this shit, I tell myself. Too old to be fighting with
young idiots in alleys. Too old to spend my night drinking whiskey till I fall
out. But the whiskey was to keep my sanity and the fights were because the
whiskey made me a little crazy.

The phone rang again and I lurched toward it.

I jerked the receiver up to my ear. "What do you want," I barked into the
phone.

"You need to get down here," a gruff voice answered.

"Yeah, and who the fuck are you?" I asked trying not to slur my words.
I still had a little bit of a buzz left over from the night before and I was real
grateful for that.

"This is Joe Briggs," the voice answered back. "I'll be in the squad room
at my desk till about noon. Come in." With that he hung up.

I wonder what he wants, I asked myself, knowing Joe Briggs never
called without having a good reason to do so.

I pick up my trail of clothes, reach inside my boxer shorts, walk to the closet, and scratch my balls. I open the closet door and drop the clothes on the pile that tumbled out on my feet when I open the door. After kicking the pile a few times, it fits in the closet again. So I close the door.

I might just do my laundry today, I think. Yeah and I just might win the lottery if I buy a ticket.

I get a table spoon and put water in it. Then carefully set it in the freezer so that the water doesn't spill out. Should've done that last night.

In the shower I saw that my ribs on both sides were bruised purple. So was my stomach. My right arm had a purple band across it where I blocked a kick. I was going to be real tender for a while, but I didn't have any broken bones. Thank God for small favors, right?

The hot water felt good. I kept it as hot as I could stand it. Which was real hot. It loosened up my muscles and helps me wake up more.

I dressed and shaved. The shiner on my left eye looked like hell. It was a big blue lump. Looked like I was trying to grow another eye right next to my left one.

I go to the icebox and get the spoon out of the freezer. The water is frozen in it. This is gonna hurt, I know. In front of the bathroom mirror, I put the bottom of the spoon to the swelling around my eye and try to push it away from the eye and flatten it. Doing it sends sharp pain screeching through my head. But I do it anyway.

I squeeze the blood around under the skin and flatten the lump somewhat.

The operation is not a total success but at least I can see a little bit better.

*　　*　　*

When I walked into The 15th Precinct where Joe Briggs worked, I was met by the same chaos that goes on there twenty-four hours a day.

There were handcuffed criminals or victims or witnesses at desks giving statements to different cops who were typing and asking questions.

Phones rang off and on all over the place. The voices were a blended blur all around me. A dozen of them, but I didn't really hear anything that was said. I made my way across the big room weaving between desks and tried not to notice anyone or be noticed.

At Joe Briggs' desk he was talking to a big fat black woman who looked like she was wearing a floral print tablecloth for a dress. He glanced up at me.

"Well Ma'am," he said with his usual poker face. "We'll keep a look out for this guy who raped your little doggie. Have the patrolmen keep their eyes open for some guy eye'n up little dogs. Can't let this kind of thing keep going on."

"No we can't," the woman said standing. "It's traumatized my little ba-by."

"I'd recommend you keep Sneekers inside from now on. There are too many freaks in the world for defenseless pups these days. You have a nice day now." The woman left.

Joe Briggs had the size, build, and skin tone of George Foreman in his forties. He was a big man but he could move frighteningly fast when he was provoked. I'd seen some guy go crazy in the precinct house one day. Joe had rolled over the guy like an avalanche. When Joe was done, which took less than a minute, the guy looked like a whole mountain had fallen on him.

In the face, Joe Briggs looked like James Earl Jones except that he never smiled. Not once had I ever seen Joe Briggs smile. The job that Joe did was hard on a man and it was a lot harder for a man with a sense of decency. Joe was a good man but the lines between good and evil sometimes get erased. I think he wasn't always sure which side of the line he was on, but he knew where he wanted to be.

Me, I could give a shit about what was good or evil. I leave that to the priests to figure out.

Joe stood up. "Let's walk," he said and headed for the front door.

I followed him.

Outside the building on the damp sidewalk walking in the drizzle, Joe glanced at my face. "You look like hell," he said.

"I feel worse than I look," I answered.

"Good," he replied.

We walked on down the street.

"Interesting case you got back there buddy," I said.

"Yeah, dog rapist. Great," he said and stepped over the steel grate to a drain. "Let me make something clear," Joe said, looking at the swirling water. "You and me, we ain't buddies."

Joe fished around in his jacket pocket with his right hand. He looked past me down the street, then over his shoulder back where we had just come from.

People were doing their normal business going in and out of shops with steel bars outside the windows. No one was near us.

Joe brought something out of his pocket, held between his thumb and finger, and held it out to me to see.

My heart skipped three beats.

It was the silencer from my thirty-eight. I suddenly knew that I hadn't even given a thought to losing it. The night I iced Morris West, I had wanted to get home and get wasted so bad nothing else mattered.

Joe spoke soft, almost a whisper, but what he said I couldn't have heard any better had he screamed it in my ear.

"You're getting real sloppy," he said. "You better get your act together, or you ain't of use to me or anyone."

Joe opened his hand and let the glued together washers fall through the grate and splash into the water below.

"Understand this," he said. "I'm like the garbage man around here. Trying to get the garbage off these streets so decent people can live. You're barely above the garbage, getting closer every day. As long as you remove garbage and as long as you're useful to me, we coexist. But if you ever hurt one of my decent people or make yourself a problem for me, I'll remove you myself." With that he turned to walk back to the police department.

"Wait a minute," I said almost shouting after him, "What's the story on the woman you sent to me, Julia Richardson?"

He stopped turned and looked at me. "She needs help. Help her if you can. Story closed."

"You're the police," I said. "Why don't you help her?"

"We've got too many cases now. I've got five unsolved murders not counting West and my worst case ain't even a murder. I'm trying to track down three real stupid strong arm men who kidnapped a parish priest in front of his family. Took him out to a barn, broke his leg with a bat and tried to saw off his ear with a knife too dull to do it with. They told him he owes their boss five thousand dollars for cocaine he bought and they'd be back to collect or kill his wife and kids. The priest is as clean as falling snow, so we know they're after the wrong guy. But that won't stop them from killing his family. We got to catch them before they do."

"Well," I said. "We all got problems, but what the hell am I supposed to do for this woman? I don't know shit about detective work and you know it."

"You know the bad people in this town and if something bad happened to her daughter, I'd bet one of them did it. Besides, charge her what you're worth and she can definitely pay your bill."

He turned to walk away, and then turned back to me. Joe looked in my eyes, "You can never repay for Kira," he said. "Not how she lived, not how she died. So you need to pay. Start by helping this woman."

CHAPTER 9
JULIA'S HOUSE

Time to try and be a detective, I tell myself and decide to go to Julia Richardson's house. She lives over on Third Street. I cruise slowly across town in my Olds.

It's not too bad over here. Houses are run down but at least there aren't as many drunks and junkies wondering the streets and you do see kids playing out on the sidewalks. I'm gonna like seeing Julia. She's a damn good lookin woman.

I can just imagine what her dark legs look like without that dress on. Long, muscular and lean.

I can imagine what she could do with those African thighs of hers too.

Wonder what kind of fur she's got between her legs. Whether it's that brillo pad type some black chicks have or if she has those loose soft curls. I'd like to find out.

I pass a familiar 7-Eleven that sells single roses at the counter.

I go in and select a large red rose from the vase and buy it.

It looks to me like a large red teardrop on a stem.

I walk about a half a block and cross the street to a small graveyard.

The low wrought iron fence is rusted. It was originally painted black.

Some of the rods were missing from the fence and some of the sections of the fence were gone altogether.

The gate shrieked of pain when I pushed it open. The drizzle blew in my face and the wind blew through the bare leafless skeletal trees.

I walked through a graveyard of forgotten people where at least half of the headstones had been kicked over and trash blew by on the wind.

Through this place of forgotten graves, I walked and stood before the grave of one who I would never forget.

I looked at the headstone with the rose in my hand. The red teardrop.

It read simply, "Kira Brooks, Rest in Peace."

I stood there. I couldn't believe that that was all that was left.

I dropped the rose on the grave.

"I'm sorry, Babe," I said. A tear ran down my cheek. Then I left.

*   *   *

Julia Richardson's house was a contrast to those that stood around it. It was a small white two bedroom home with a shingled roof. The lawn was well maintained. The yard was free of trash and there was a family of decorative plastic ducks in the middle of the lawn. There were two large man sized bushes on both sides of the front door.

The house looked to be well taken care of. The paint was not cracked or chipped, relatively fresh. The curtains were a soft yellow. They looked bright against the surrounding drabness of the rundown neighborhood. Completely around the house there was a white picket fence.

This was Julia's oasis and sanctuary from the hard world that surrounds her.

I went up to the front door and knocked. There was no answer.

There was no garage on the side of the house and no car parked in front. All indications were that there was no one home.

Well, I guess I picked up on that one real quick. I'm beginning to turn into a regular Sherlock Holmes.

I knock again, just for the hell of it and just as I stop, a brown Pinto Wagon pulls up.

Julia Richardson gets out of the car and hurries up the walk toward me.

She's wearing hospital whites and looking good in them too. Her eyes ask the question I have no answer for so instead I say, "I need to look around Felicia's room. See if I can find a direction to take this investigation in."

Julia was unlocking the door.

"Don't know what good that'll do," she said. "I know who Felicia's friends are and none of them know where she's at."

Julia opened the door and flipped on the light switch. I followed her inside. Julia went to the kitchen.

The house was simply furnished but it was neat and clean. Everything appeared to be in its proper place.

There was a bookshelf with an old set of encyclopedias in it and assorted paperbacks that range from Stephen King and Dean Koontz to Stephen Baldwin and Maya Angelou. There was an old console stereo. The kind that played record albums on a turntable.

Looking at the albums that were beside the console, I saw that there was a lot of old blues like Billie Holliday and Leadbelly. I saw a lot of rhythm and blues and soul too. I liked a lot of these guys myself.

Talking loudly enough for Julia to hear me from the kitchen in the next room I said, "I see you like Teddy Pendergrass." She had seven of his albums.

Julia stuck her head through the doorway. There was a twinkle in her eyes and a certain huskiness to her voice.

"Listen," she said, "That there was a man. Don't nobody mess with my Teddy Bear in this house. That is sacrilege."

From back in the kitchen she asked, "Do you want something to drink?"

"Take a shot of whiskey," I answered.

She laughed. It was a good sound, loose and giggly. "Not here," she said. "Don't keep it. We got milk, lemonade or ice tea."

"Milk will probably kill me," I told her. "Better make it ice tea."

We drank ice tea together. I sat on the couch and she sat in an easy chair.

"What happened to your eye?" Julia asked, "You forget to duck?"

"It was a sucker punch," I told her. "And you should've seen the other guys when I was done."

"Anyone who gets hit is a sucker," Julia said matter-of-factly. "And I don't care who won. You shouldn't have been doin what you were doin."

"You don't know the whole story," I said.

"Don't need to," she cut me off. "I've heard stories by the best and if you think you're going to enlighten me about the ways of the world, you're late."

We both burst out laughing.

"Damn, you're a tough woman," I said, "You always this nice to every-one who comes to your home?"

"Only when they need it," Julia said.

We sipped the tea and made idle talk until Julia looked at her watch. She said, "I don't mean to rush you but I need to be in bed soon."

My eyebrows involuntarily raised.

"Don't even think it," Julia said. "All men are boys and I ain't nobody's playground. I'm working a split shift today so I need some sleep."

"No need to explain," I said with a crooked smile on my face while standing.

"Damn right there ain't," she said and led me into Felicia's room.

*　　*　　*

The room that Felicia lived in was typical of girls her age, but it was uniquely her own as well.

Black teenage heartthrobs covered the walls. Michael Jordan was up there and so was Michael Jackson from back when he still looked human.

The bed was covered with teddy bears and other stuffed animals. Over the headboard of the bed was a framed, fierce looking picture of Bobby Fisher studying a chessboard. Under the picture on white wide hospital tape, Felicia had boldly printed, "Never, Ever, Consider Surrender."

I hadn't even met this kid but I liked her already.

Julia saw me looking at the picture and its caption. "That's the way she plays," Julia told me. "Felicia will never resign a chess game, even when the game is hopeless she hangs on so she can exhaust her opponent for the next game. I really think she could be one of the best in the world."

Felicia had a chest of drawers with a dresser and a large mirror beside it. On top of the chest of drawers was an Aztec style granite chess set. Pieces and squares were pink and black.

It wasn't expensive but it was a beautiful set.

On the dresser was a Kasparov computer chess set.

"Felicia beats that thing all the time," Julia said, obviously proud. "I can't even touch it at the lowest levels but Felicia tears it up at the hardest."

I looked at Julia and said, "Tell me about the morning you knew Felicia was gone."

Julia took a deep breath. "Not much to tell really," she said. "I was working a split that night like tonight. I go to work at ten and get off at six. Felicia had just finished her homework and was ready for bed. I gave her a hug and went to work. Next morning I get home about six fifteen, she's gone and her bedroom window is open." Julia pointed to one of two windows in the room.

I went to the window and inspected it. Trying to look like I actually knew what I was doing. The window was latched. I tried to move it up to see if the screws were loose. They weren't.

"Are these windows always latched?" I asked.

"Always locked," Julia replied.

I opened the window and looked out at the ground below. It was roughly five and a half feet to the ground. No problem for someone to climb in or out. The ground was covered with thick brownish grass. Thick enough so no footprints would have been made.

I turned away from the window. Nothing to be learned there.

I looked in Julia's eyes. "I don't like to ask this," I said. "But, do you mind if I look through your daughter's things?"

She looked at the floor then back in my eyes. There was almost moistness there. "I don't like it," she said. "But I guess it's necessary."

I took an ink pen from my pocket and went to the chest of drawers and opened the drawer.

Just socks in there and some tee shirts. I moved them around with the ink pen making tapping and scraping noises as I was doing it. I didn't know what I was looking for. Just something unusual. I was glad I didn't find any indication of drug use.

The chest of drawers yielded nothing more than clothes and a couple magazines of *Young Miss*. On the second drawer down in the dresser, I

33

noticed that the sound of my pen tapping on the wood at the bottom changed. On impulse I pulled it out and felt underneath.

A book was taped to the bottom.

*　　*　　*

"What's that?" Julia asked as I pulled the book loose from the tape holding it in place.

I showed it to her. A black journal with dates on each page and entrees for each day. Nothing unusual, but there were letters between some of the pages.

"I've never seen that before," Julia said. And I did find that unusual.

"I'm going to need to read this," I told Julia. "I know a diary's personal, so no one will see this but me."

"Well, I'm going to say it again," Julia said. "I don't like it, but I guess it is necessary."

I looked through the other drawers and through Felicia's closet and found nothing that you wouldn't expect to find in any sixteen-year-old girl's room. Then we went back to the living room.

Julia led me to her front door in silence. We stopped there. I looked at her face.

"I didn't like having to look through Felicia's stuff," I told her.

"I didn't like letting you," she said. "I've always respect Felicia's privacy. But I guess I can't right now."

"I hope I can find something so I can get her back to you."

"I hope so too," Julia said and I gave her a hug. Just a man comforting a woman with a lost child.

CHAPTER 10
THE COLD WORLD

My car is cold.

My world is cold.

I cruise slowly down the streets of East St. Louis and I can't get the thought of Julia out of my mind. A good woman who trusts me.

And what am I? If she knew me she wouldn't trust me.

Julia is a woman who raises her child the best way she can. She fights against the cruelty and chaos of the world by just being who she is. A good loving mother.

Me, I'm a part of the chaos. I make my money by removing problems that the police have no legitimate way of dealing with. When the police have a drug dealer, a murderer, a rapist or anyone who is so bad that he just has to go but the police can't prosecute him, they call me. They pay me to remove their problem. They don't care how; they just want it done.

Morris West was a freebie. I just hated that son of a bitch and this is my neighborhood. But he wasn't the first and he won't be the last.

Julia felt warm in my arms. Warmth was all around her. In her skin, in her heart and in her home. A good place to live. A warm place to live.

I live in the cold.

My world is cold. It's where I belong. It's where I deserve to be.

My first trash removal was a freebie too.

*   *   *

It was four years ago when I needed some money bad and my former methods of making money were closed to me. I didn't have the heart to deal anymore. Just couldn't make myself do it. The athletic commission took my boxing license after I axe-kicked a guy in a boxing match. So no prize fighting anymore.

My rent was way overdue. The electric was close to being shut off. I had a funeral and a grave to pay for. They don't bury the people you love for free.

What the hell was I gonna do? Go to work for McDonalds? The only thing I knew how to do good was kill and the army wasn't about to take me back.

Then Marco Rios knocked on my door.

We both sat down at my table and when my former supplier broke out a joint and offered it to me, I said, "I don't want any."

"That's all right," Marcos said in his smooth Latin voice, "I understand. More for me anyway. Besides, I need it."

Then he proceeded to tell me about his daughter, Lisa, running away from home. He advanced me two thousand dollars to look for her, against ten thousand dollars for when I brought her home.

It wasn't too much of a problem finding out where Lisa Rios had run off to. All I had to do was offer some money for information. I knew the guys she had been going around with so for about a hundred dollars, I was able to get hold of a phone number where she was at.

Getting her home wasn't easy.

When I called the phone number, I got a Paco (first name only) in a cheap hotel in Kansas City. He said that Marco's daughter was with him.

We negotiated.

Paco agreed to sell her to me for one thousand dollars.

We agreed to meet at an abandoned grade school in Independence, Missouri about twenty miles east of Kansas City. Like an idiot I agreed to every condition that Paco set and I played by his rules totally. I would never do that kind of thing again.

After driving the two hundred and fifty miles to Independence, I parked my car a block and a half from Harris Elementary School. I hid my gun and five hundred dollars under the back seat. Then I went to the school with fourteen hundred dollars in my pocket.

Harris School had a tall fence around it with barbed wire at the top. It looked like a deserted reform school with the wire mesh in the windows and the huge oak doors.

On the door hung a condemned sign and "Keep Out" was below it.

I entered the school yard at a section of the fence where wire cutters had been used to make a big hole. Trash was blowing around the school in little whirlpools of dust and cigarette pack wrappers, and I saw on the side of the schoolhouse a gymnasium where I had been told it would be.

I walked to the gymnasium side door. The wind blew dust up in my face and I felt a lot like Jimmy Stewart in *High Noon*, except I left my gun in the car. I was feeling really naked without it.

A saying I had used throughout my life was "Mamma Dark never raised no idiots". Well with every step I took towards that gymnasium door with fourteen hundred dollars in one pocket and no gun in the other pocket to protect it with, I was feeling like I had been lying. But it was too late now.

I pushed the door open. The metal door screeched like an old male cat getting his balls stepped on. I stepped into the big gymnasium hall. My footsteps echoed hollowly in the big room. They, five of them not counting Marco's daughter, were sitting on fold out bleachers. They watched me approach. Two of them high-fived each other a loud slap.

The five stood up simultaneously and formed a semicircle around me.

Lisa Rios had a jittery frightened look on her face. Her eyes were red and swollen. Whether from crying or being slapped, I couldn't tell. She was small and looked to be around fourteen years old. She looked like she had a real rough time of it since running away. Bet she wished she were at home with good old mom and pops right now.

"You told me we'd meet alone," I told the leader of the band of merry men who I guessed was Paco.

He laughed, "Well, I guess I ain't as fuckin stupid as you are."

I guess he was right about that.

Paco was a sweaty looking Mexican with a pock marked face and acted a hell of a lot like Al Pacino in Scarface. The other four, two Mexicans and two Blacks looked like escapees from a mental hospital that specialized in violent psychotics.

I looked past Paco at Lisa Rios and she met my eyes. Tears had started leaking from the corner of her eyes and there was a silent pleading there. "You choose your playmates real well," I told her.

Paco spoke with a low guttural raspy voice, "Meet my playmate". He pulled a chrome plated forty-five, shoved the barrel five inches from my face.

Nice gun, I thought, *who'd you steal that from.*

"Say hello to my little friend," Paco hissed.

I'd seen that movie too. "Can't you be more original," I said.

Paco smiled, he had rotten teeth and the breath to match.

"Tie him up," he said.

One produced a cord from his pocket; two held my arms tight behind me while my hands were tied together.

The gun was still in my face. I knew better than to even flinch. One finger twitch from Paco and my face would be undercooked hamburger.

He lowered the gun when my hands were tied tight.

"We can still do the deal," I told Paco. "If anything happens to Lisa or me, Marco will have you killed."

Paco still had that smile on his face, "This is my jungle," he said and kicked me in the balls.

Pain exploded up through my body and I went to my knees. Someone punched or kicked me in the head and I went to the floor on my side.

All five were laughing now. A psychotic giggling.

"She says her Daddy don't give a fuck," Paco said, then in a little girl's voice he sing-songed, "Momma don't love me, Daddy don't love me no more." Then he said harshly, "Bring the stupid bitch to me."

One of the others dragged Lisa by her hair down the bleachers and across the floor. She tried to walk but was jerked off her feet three times so he could drag her.

Paco grabbed me by the hair and pulled me to a sitting position.

"You are a stupid son of a bitch," Paco said and punched me in the mouth. He couldn't hit hard; it was like something my grandmother might have thrown.

I laughed. He punched me again. I laughed some more.

He slung me by my hair sideways to the floor. "You fuckhead," he yelled and kicked me in the back. It hurt like hell but I laughed anyway. I figured, he's gonna kill me no matter what, so I might as well piss him off. These little Hitler types were all the same. They gotta prove over and over again what bad ass big men they are because they don't really believe it themselves. So I laughed just to piss him off. And it worked.

"You gonna laugh motherfucker," he screamed at me, going red in the face, and kicked me again. I kept laughing and I noticed then that the cord I was tied with was rubber and it was stretching.

Paco stepped away from me and handed the chrome forty-five to one of his boys. "Watch him," he said. Then he walked to where Lisa lay sobbing on the floor unzipping his fly as he did.

Paco reached down and grabbed Lisa by her hair and jerked her to her knees. "Suck my dick, bitch," he barked at her. She hesitated and he slapped her hard, creating a loud pop that echoed through the gym. Then she did what she was told.

The other four guy's eyes were glued to what Paco was doing to the little girl.

One of them said, "I wanna be next. I want me some of dat." They started arguing about who was gonna be next.

I tried to sit up working the cords as I did. I was kicked back to lying on my side.

No one was watching me so I worked on my cords, straining and stretching them.

The others, including the one who was supposed to be watching me, had formed a circle around Paco and Lisa and was cheering Paco on with "Fuck her face man! Yeah, fuck that bitch!"

Paco was gripping the back of Lisa's head and was shoving his dick at her so hard she was making gagging noises. Then one of the others said something about her having more than one hole to fill and they were ripping her clothes off of her. The girl was whimpering and crying but they didn't care. One of them started fucking her from behind and grunting as he was doing it like a hog.

Then I got my hands loose. The first one that saw me on my feet was the one with the gun. But it was too late for him. I jammed a left jab in his Adams apple and wrenched the gun from his hand as I stomped on his foot. He grabbed his throat and bent forward. I shoved the barrel of the gun in his left eye socket and blew the back of his head all over Paco's back.

One of the two blacks, a short guy, hadn't been doing hardly anything but just standing and staring. Now he was just backing up with his hands in the air, mouthing a word I couldn't hear that sounded something like "Op, op." But I'm no lip reader and he wasn't a threat so I went after the others.

The one who had been fucking Lisa from behind was trying to hop away and put his pants up at the same time. I put a bullet in his ass hoping it would come out through his dick.

The other one tried to rush me. I put a bullet in his throat. When he went to his knees, I made a big ragged red hole appear where his nose had been.

Lisa was flat on her face covering her ears with her hands and Paco was standing staring at me with his mouth wide open and his dick hanging out.

My ears were ringing but I was beginning to hear again. I realized right then that the loud shots from the gun had momentarily deafened me, but I couldn't even remember what they sounded like.

I could hear good enough to hear the guy who had been backing off say, "I'm a cop."

I looked at him and he bent down and slowly took out of his sock a Police ID and held it out to me.

"Now you take it easy," he said.

I saw the flicker of a shit-eating grin cross Paco's face. I looked at Paco with his hands in the air and his dick hanging out.

"Fuck you," I said and shot Paco's dick off. He screamed and went to his knees. The look of horror on his face was priceless. Then I shot him in the forehead.

"Oh shit," I heard the guy say who I now knew was a cop, "We got a big problem."

"Not me," I told him, "You do."

* * *

Right after I got Lisa Rios to her feet and dressed as well as we could with what was left of her clothes, four guys came bursting through the door with their guns drawn.

"Hold it right there," one of them yelled to Lisa and me.

"You're a little late," I said.

"Put the gun down," he yelled, taking a firing stance and pointing his gun at me.

"Fuck you," I told him, realizing I still held the chrome forty-five so I put it in my jacket pocket.

Lisa was still sobbing. She put her face in my chest. I pushed Lisa behind me. Pointed my finger at the face of the idiot with his gun on me.

"If you don't put that gun down," I told him. "I'm gonna shove it up your ass."

I took a step toward him.

"Stand down Franklin," I heard a voice command and the cop put his gun away. Up stepped one of the four, a man with graying hair and a commanding presence.

"Nash Graham," he said and extended his hand. "DEA"

"John Dark," I said and instantly added, "Private Investigator."

"Ugly work," he said smiling.

"Always is," I answered.

He slapped me on the back, "There's always more work like this," he said. "A talented man can make a lot of money. Are you interested?"

"Yeah," I told him.

The guy I'd ass-shot moved and said he needed a doctor.

"A problem," Nash said, "We got a witness."

I took the forty-five out, took aim at ass-shot guy's head and blew a chunk out of it. He moaned no more.

"Now we don't," I told Nash.

Nash laughed and said to the other DEA agents, "I like this guy."

So that was how I got into the shit I'm into now.

How could a woman like Julia Richardson want to know a guy like me? Since that day in Independence, Missouri, I've killed more people than I can count on my fingers and toes and I like it. It gets me off like nothing else. As long as they pay me, I do the job. More for the harder ones but all of them are really just the same to me.

How could a woman like Julia want me? Her of the warm home, of the warm heart. Me a burned out killer. Why would she want me and could she ever love me?

Love? Fuck that. I just want to stick my dick in her. She don't know what's she's missing.

CHAPTER 11
POEMS AND PROSTITUTES

I pulled myself enough out of my trip down memory lane to realize I was cruising about a block and a half away from Johnny's Bar and Grill. I decided to go there to have a look at the diary I'd found in Felicia Richardson's room. Then a bit of the past intruded upon the present again.

It was Lisa Rios standing on the corner.

She smiled and waved. I waved back. Now she could be had for twenty dollars or a rock of crack cocaine. You see, after I got her home, I found out dear old daddy, Marco Rios, had wanted her home for more reasons than to just be a good father to his daughter.

Marco had been fucking his own daughter ever since she had looked big enough to be able to handle it. The next time she ran away from home she was over eighteen so the dogs weren't called out to chase her. By then it was too late.

Now she just sells her body cheap and uses the money to buy crack to deaden her pain. A word like love doesn't exist for her because the one person she thought she could trust and love used her.

She's offered to do me for free anytime I want, but I just can't bring myself to touch her. There's just too much sadness there.

I guess I'd rather remember the little girl who could still be hurt rather than know the confused woman with skin like steel.

And for that psychological breakdown, Oprah Winfrey would be proud.

So I got out of the car and walked into Johnny's. I really needed a drink and I really needed to read this diary.

*　　*　　*

"Oh shit," Johnny says as I walk toward the bar, "Here comes trouble, lock the doors."

Then he leans to the side and takes a long look at my black eye.

"Looks like trouble already found you," he says, "Woo- that looks pretty. You ought a get your ass whipped every day. Helps us not notice the rest of your ugly face."

"Thanks," I said, "I needed that."

"Just tryin to help ya," he said.

I ordered a Budweiser, took a drink, sat on a barstool and took out Felicia's diary.

Johnny and the same silent drunk that was in the bar yesterday was watching reruns of *Leave It To Beaver*.

"How come you watch that shit?" I ask Johnny.

"It reminds me how stupid white folks are," Johnny tells me. "Check this out. June Cleaver is always telling Ward, 'Hey go easy on the Beaver.' Shit, old June ain't bad lookin in an okeydokey sort of a way. If she were my old lady, she'd be beggin me to pound the Beaver morning, noon, and night. Wouldn't be no 'Take it easy on the Beaver,' if I was on the job."

"You amaze me," I told Johnny, "You wanna fuck everything on TV."

"That's right," he says, "I'll fuck em all."

The drunk, who hadn't spoken in so long, I didn't know he could speak, spoke now. "His favorite show is Mr. Ed," he said clearly, even though he was falling off his stool drunk.

I laughed and said, "Guess that horse looks pretty good."

"Just like your mamma," Johnny answered and laughed.

I started reading the diary, which started at the beginning of the year and ended the day before Felicia vanished. I skimmed through a lot of the stuff she'd written because it was just girl's stuff like - school, tests, what guys were cute, who was going with who, what girls had gotten pregnant and just general gossip.

I came to a page that I found might have something useful about the same time that Johnny said he wanted me to watch the bar so he could bring back some food for us.

He wouldn't bring back my White Castle burgers. Said I'd stunk up the john too much last time I'd eaten them. He's probably right. I love the taste of them but they run right through me. So he went for Kentucky Fried Chicken and I went behind the bar and continued reading Felicia's diary.

This is the first page where I found a mention of something unusual in her life. It was about three months ago.

. . . Played in the chess tournament today. Kicked Ass! Oops, Mom would make me say I scored a profound triumph. I like Kicked Ass better!

That white boy almost cried when he realized it was hopeless. I love it when they resign. I felt like jumping and screaming. But I didn't. That wouldn't be ladylike. Mom says I gotta be a lady.

Something spooky today.

Some guy was staring at me through the whole tournament. He dressed like he's rich and he might be kind of cute except he's so Old, Old, Old!!! Christ I think he's over 30. Yuck!!!

When he looked at me it made me feel like I had a bug on my neck. Yuck!!!. . .

There were a few pages of gossip and stuff like that. Then she went to a chess tournament in Bethalto.

. . . He was watching me again. A coal black guy. He looked slick in this three-piece suit . . .

Felicia's attitude seemed to be changing toward this watcher. She wasn't calling him spooky now.

. . . He was staring at me. Smiling at me. His eyes are penetrating like he looks in my soul . . .

Several more times she wrote of him at chess tournaments. Then he made a stronger overture than just a look after a tournament.

. . . He passed me a note today. God what a romantic. . .

Between the pages of the journal at this point there was a folded piece of paper, a poem. It read.

> You move the pieces
> And they all watch
> But only I understand
> They do not see

You are their queen
They are pawns
In your hand
The King

Pretty lame poem, I thought. But what was really important was what Felicia had thought about it. She wrote:

. . . Poem was cute. He doesn't seem like such a bad guy, just real lonely...

Made me feel like Felicia must be real lonely. I thought about it and realized that without Felicia having a father or any male around her at home on a regular basis, she must feel a need for a father figure of some sort. That left her particularly vulnerable to the kind of freak this asshole was. Made me want to twist this guy's head off. Julia couldn't help the fact that she didn't have a husband. There just weren't too many good men around in East St. Louis to choose from. And this asshole was going to take advantage of a little girl because of that.

. . . He talked to me today. He's not like the boys at school. He knows things. He's a man . . .

There was another piece of folded paper between the pages. Another poem:

There is so much
There is no way of knowing
That I can teach
What level you can reach
I will come to you
And take you there
Forever, Forever
We will walk on air
The King

This guy is a sick puppy no doubt about it. I decided right then that I was going to be the cure for his sickness.

On the next page there were comments about another chess tournament. This one at The Fairview Heights High School. Then there was:

. . . He was there again tonight. We talked after the tournament. He really seems like he listens to me. And when he looks at me it really seems like he sees me like I see me. He says he's going to visit me at home after Mom is at work some night . . .

That was Felicia's last entry.

I'm guessing that he did visit her and took her with him. I didn't know how I was going to find Felicia and this freak, but I knew I had to.

So all I had was a description and a real vague one at that.

He's maybe thirty years old, dresses rich, and has coal black skin and penetrating eyes.

That fits about half the black guys in East St. Louis except for the clothes and those can be changed. What I had was nothing.

* * *

Leave It To Beaver had gone off and *Lost In Space* was about half over when the drunk at the bar told me to give him a beer for free.

I told him nothing is free in life, so he gave me the finger, said I was a cheap bastard and staggered out the door.

A few minutes later, Johnny walked in carrying a bucket of chicken. Coming in after Johnny was that kid who had been with the two idiots who jumped me the night before.

"Well, ain't this a fuckin treat," I said and started around the bar.

"Hold on a minute there," Johnny said with his hand in the air motioning me to stop. "Terry is a kid and there's something he wants to say to you."

I came around the bar and told Johnny, "If he's old enough to run with the two assholes who jumped me, he's old enough to take the same kind of ass whippin I gave them. Unless he gives me a good reason not to."

"Look man," Terry said. "I don't really even know those guys. That was the first time I'd even hung out with them. If they jumped you, I'm sorry but I didn't have anything to do with it. Hell, man, I was out of there right when they tried to pull that shit here."

Johnny sat the bucket of chicken down on a table. "So are you going to be peaceful or am I going to have to beat you with a chicken leg," he said to me.

I sat down and pulled off the top of the bucket. Johnny sat down. Terry remained standing.

"Well sit down, "I told him motioning him to a chair." I'm too god-damned hungry to argue. And I figure I ain't gonna be safe around here until I eat these four legs."

After we'd all eaten a couple pieces of the Colonial's greasiest, I told Terry I was looking for a kid he might know and showed him Felicia's picture.

"Yeah I know Felicia," Terry said. "I've been wonderin why she wasn't in school. I was gonna go by her house, but I don't think her mom likes me."

So I told him about Felicia's disappearance.

"Look man," Terry said with his face set real serious. "I really like Felicia. She's real nice. I even asked her out once. Her mother said no. So look, if there's any way I can help you to get her back home, just let me know."

I told him I would.

"You know," he said. "Felicia's mom is all right but she should've gave me a chance, ya know. I would've treated Felicia right. She's really special, ya know."

"Julia is the kind of woman," I told Terry. "That you'll have to prove yourself special before you get a chance with her daughter."

"I guess you're right," Terry said.

We ate more chicken. Johnny and I drank a couple of Budweiser's. Terry drank a coke.

Star Trek came on. Johnny talked about Uhuru's ass under that short skirt. *Star Trek* went off.

A couple of local guys came in. They rolled dice with Johnny on the bar.

A bad idea. He beat them for about thirty dollars apiece before they got disgusted and left.

About eight thirty, Terry got up to leave. Again he offered to help to find Felicia.

I told him I'd keep him in mind. He left.

Some other local guys came in and started playing dice with Johnny.

He knows better than to ask me to play. I've already lost too much money to him to play him anymore.

I don't mind it that Johnny cheats at dice. It's just that he's so damn good at it that I can never catch him at it that bothers me.

Somebody started playing the jukebox. It was something about "a very special girl, the kind you won't take home to momma." Yeah, I thought, probably the kind I'd throw a paper bag on her head and hope it never comes off. I can't stand that kind of shit music.

So about ten, I headed home.

CHAPTER 12
GHOST'S

It's raining lightly outside. Seems like it's always raining. I get in my car and turn on the ignition. I know I'll be home before the heater is warm so I don't even bother turning it on. It's only a block anyway. I turn on the radio instead.

Elton John is singing *Someone Saved My Life Tonight*. As I drive home I think about Terry and the look on his face when he talked about Felicia. There was a yearning and a hunger and something else indescribable, the need for a man to be better than he is and to do it for someone else. Maybe Terry, in his own teenage high school way, was in love with Felicia. He sure wanted to look good in her eyes, I could tell that.

Not so long ago, I could have been like that. I could have been the kind of guy who would accomplish great things for a woman that I loved. But I've lost that now. Now I'm hollow.

Kira, I could have saved your life that night. I should have saved you from me.

With you gone, who's gonna save me now? It probably doesn't even matter, since I'm already dead.

*   *   *

In my apartment I turn on the TV and head to the icebox. I have about half of a quart bottle of Ancient Age whiskey left over.

That should do the job. I should have learned long ago to not let myself think about Kira any time after dark.

Not if I plan on sleeping that night.

But the Ancient Age should do the trick. Maybe Kira's ghost will sleep tonight.

I check my bruises in the mirror. They're fading a little bit. But my ribs are still tender. The swelling around my eye has gone down. But it's still purple.

What the hell. I can see and that's what matters.

While I lay on my couch the TV spoke to me. On the news good old President Ronnie Reagan told me how to be a better American.

I took a big drink of Ancient Age. Jesus, it tasted as old as its name said it was. I looked at Reagan, the wrinkled old fuck, and said, "Fuck you Ronald. Why don't you go back to *Death Valley Days* and take the Rawhide from Bonzo right up your ass. As if you know what America is really like. You don't know shit."

I changed the channel.

M.A.S.H. is on. "Fuck you Hawkeye." I change the channel. *Mork And Mindy* is on. "Nannew Nannew you fuckin idiot." I change the channel again.

All right, there he is. There's my boy. *Psycho* is coming on. Norman Bates, my hero, is walking down the steps of the Bates Motel. I like Norman. If there's anybody more fucked up than me it's Norman.

I take a big harsh drink of Ancient Age and settle back to watch.

Norman, what a well-adjusted guy.

The whiskey is soothing my brain. Good! I blink my eyes watching Norman rent a room to a victim.

He looks directly at me. Holding the key out to me. He says, "For you John." The set goes blank, only snow and the white noise of static.

Kira Brooks walks into the room from the kitchen with a big bowl of popcorn in her hands.

I jump up from the couch.

"What's up with you," she says. "Is the movie on yet?"

She sets the popcorn down on the coffee table. I go to her and take her in my arms and hold her to me. I'm crying. I can't stop it. Tears are running down my face.

"What's the matter baby?" she asks and I look in her deep black eyes. I touch the chocolate skin of her cheek with my fingertips.

"I thought you were dead," I tell her and kiss her soft lips. "I thought I'd lost you and I didn't want to live, but I didn't have a choice."

"Oh Baby," she said in her husky sexy voice. "Don't worry. It's just a bad dream, just a dream. I'm here to take care of you."

I wiped my tears away. "I just don't know what I'd do without you," I told her. "I know I don't say it enough but I love you." And I held her close as we walked to the bedroom.

"Honey," Kira whispered in my ear like a frightened child. "Will you please quit dealing? You know I can't handle the cocaine. The only way I can stay away from it is for you to get rid of what we got and quit dealin."

"Sure Baby," I tell her and she breathes heavy as I kiss her neck. "I'll sell what I got," I say as I unbutton her blouse and kiss her breasts. "Then I'll quit dealin. I'll have enough money to quit."

I know I'm lying even as I pull her blue jeans off of her slim legs and she pulls my clothes off me.

"You promise," Kira says and moans as I rub my face on the skin between her legs and then on her stomach.

"I promise," I tell her and pull her panties off and throw them.

Kira's breathing harsh now. "You'll get rid of it and not get no more," she gasps.

"Yes," I lie and I plunge myself into her.

She gasps and whimpers, "Oh, God thank you," and pulls me deep into her and we move together. Both of us are one rhythm.

Kira gasps and grabs me tight. She screeches, "Oh, Lord, Oh, Oh, Lord."

And I pound into her seeing her face contorted and tight.

"Oh, Lord," Kira yells then screams loud a high pitched squeal. She goes rigid. Muscles all tight and I see it. The white spots around her nostrils. The cocaine left there.

Her head is thrown back, her eyes bulging. The veins on her necks stick out. She's trembling.

"No, No, No," I scream but I know it's too late. I've lived this before.

She's in my arms and I'm inside Kira but she is dead. I can feel the heat of her draining away.

I pound on her chest but it doesn't work. She's dead. My Kira is dead.

I try CPR but she doesn't respond.

Her eyes are open, staring…dead.

I pound on her chest and yell, "No," and find myself pounding on the ground, on the dirt. I know I'm kneeling on her grave as I've done countless times since her death.

How could I let it happen?

I left my uncut cocaine in the house with the woman I loved who was addicted to it. She begged me dozens of times to quit dealing and each time I lied and told her I would.

But I never did and now it was too late.

"Oh, Kira," I said digging my fingers into the dirt. "I'm so sorry babe. I'm so sorry." Tears run down my face as my head hangs down.

The ground below me is a trembling. Then two hands shoot up from the damp earth and grasp me around the throat in a choking deadly embrace.

Kira has got me by the throat. Her arms are dry, sticks. Her face is partially eaten away. Bugs fall from where her right eye had once been. The left stares at me with hatred. She opens her mouth and maggots pour out.

"Come with me baby," she says and I feel myself dragged down below the dirt into the darkness by her claw like hands on my throat.

I try to scream but I can't breathe. I can't breathe. There's a beating in my ears, my heart pounding, pounding.

I bolt upright on the couch and I scream. But the pounding continues.

The door, the door, it's the door, I finally realize after my eyes focus a bit. Someone is pounding on the door.

I stand, my legs shaky, trying to shake the dream out of my head and go and answer the door.

PART II

TACTICS
AND
STRATEGY

Kill the body
And the head will die
- Joe Louis

The Candyman can. . .
- Sammy Davis Jr.

Out here at the bottom of the deep blue sea
The fish are never
Quite what they seem
Some of them kill
Some of them die
But no one will ever
Answer why. . .
- The Walker in Darkness

In the dark
We are all blind.
- The Walker in Darkness

CHAPTER 13
MOMMA ROSA AND SLOP CHEWY

It was Rosa Delgado at the door. I pulled the door open and she came in saying, "Wake up sleepy head."

I must have groaned because I had a horrible headache and her words felt like ice picks in both ears.

Rosa was a short, chunky, happy Spanish woman in her fifties who charged me fifty dollars a week to do my laundry and clean up my apartment.

"What time is it?" I asked Rosa.

"Noon," she said and looking the place over she made a noise like, "Ayeeieechee!" And said, "The pigs live here."

"Thanks," I said. I was still dressed in the same clothes I had worn the night before and my chest felt sticky. I think I fell asleep while taking a drink of the whiskey and spilled it all over myself.

"Tell me," Rosa says, "Are all white men as messy as you are?"

"Only when they can be," I say.

Rosa moves around the place picking things up and putting the apartment in some kind of order.

I get some clothes from the closet and walk past Rosa on the way to the bathroom.

"Whooo you smell," she says. "A Mexican man could not be as dirty as you. A Mexican woman would not let him be."

"I know Rosa," I told her. "I need a woman just like you."

"I'm too much for you," she says and laughs, "I'd wear you out."

I go in the bathroom and shave and when I close the door to take a shower, she shouts through the door, "Don't you play with yourself in there. I know all you white men are perverts."

I take five aspirins and shout back just before I step in the shower, "You love me don't you Rosa?"

"Oh yeah," she answers. "Just like I love all my dogs. You're my favorite puppy."

I like Rosa. She can get me going when I really don't feel like going.

The shower made me feel like I was almost human again, but I was still walking around in a fog. I got dressed and came out of the bathroom.

Rosa was finishing up what few dishes I had. She had already finished cleaning up the rest of the apartment and had the laundry stacked by the front door.

"Damn you're fast," I tell her.

"Too fast for you," Rosa answered.

She finished the dishes and I paid Rosa. Then I helped her carry the laundry to her family's apartment just down the hall. She knew I'd pick it up the next day.

"Don't you get in trouble tonight," Rosa told me as I was leaving.

"I won't Momma Rosa," I said.

"If I was your Momma I'd spank you," she said with a smile and closed the door.

*   *   *

I was hungry as hell and Ben Lee's Chinese House was about three blocks away. So I drove over there. The dream I'd had about Kira was still at the edge of my consciousness. It was a dream that I had over and over again. The problem wasn't that I had nightmares. Hell, most people have an occasional nightmare. It's no big deal. They fade away because we know the monsters in those dreams aren't real.

My problem was that most of these nightmares are memories. Kira did beg me over and over again to quit dealing because she was addicted to my drugs. And I had lied to her over and over again telling her I would quit dealing. Kira died while we were making love. Her heart just seized up. Near pure cocaine does that to some people.

The part of the dream that never happened, Kira coming out of the ground to grab me and drag me down with her, is a wish fulfillment thing, I think. I know it's what I deserve, but it never happens in the real world. So I make myself pay in my dreams.

Ben Lee's Chinese House was, from the outside, like most businesses in this part of East St. Louis, very uninviting. With the crime rate around here you couldn't help it. Steel wire mesh over the windows and steel security doors were necessary here for a business's survival.

But once you came through the front door it was a different story. Beautiful paintings of mountain scenes done in an oriental style covered the walls. Soft lighting and soft oriental music created an atmosphere that was romantic, relaxing, and exotic.

Lots of guys from the neighborhood brought dates here to loosen them up so they could forget about the world outside and maybe get some good loving later in the night. I came here because the food was great.

I went in and sat at a table and a pretty oriental woman in a traditional oriental dress came out to greet me. Her skin was darker than Ben Lee's. Ben Lee was Chinese but grew up in East St. Louis. She was slender and small and had a voice so soft it sounded like she was whispering.

"Hello," she said. "I am Me Ly. I will be your waitress." She placed a menu on the table with a smile that could only be described as humble.

"You Lay?" I asked.

She looked at me perplexed, "I don't understand."

"Your name," I said, "You Lay."

She laughed nervously, "Oh no, no," she said. "Me Ly, I from Korea, speak English not so good."

"Oh," I said glancing at the menu and before she had a chance to walk away I said, "Do you like Chinese food?"

"Well," Me Ly said, "I Korean, but I like Chinese food."

"Do you like Cream of Some Young Guy?" I ask Me Ly.

Again she gets that perplexed look on her face. "I might," Me Ly says pleasantly, "I not know what it is but I might like it."

"Well, go tell Ben Lee to whip you up some Cream of Some Young Guy and you can find out if you like it."

"Yes, I will," she said and walks toward the kitchen door that was only about twenty feet from where I sat. Me Ly went through the kitchen door. I hear some talking then some laughter.

About a minute later, Ben Lee comes out of the kitchen and sits down at my table.

"You're a mean guy," he tells me in a voice with no trace of an oriental accent and laughs.

"Just having some fun," I tell him and we shake hands.

Me Ly came out of the kitchen carrying a platter of food. As she passed our table, she gave me a look that was designed to make my hair burst into flame.

Ben looked at me and I looked at Ben. We both said, "Woo," simultaneously.

"She really likes you," Ben said laughing.

"Yeah, I can tell," I answered.

Ben stood up and slapped me on the shoulder, "Gotta get back to work," he said. "I had them put on some beef curry and chicken fried rice for ya. I know you like that."

"So now I don't even get to order here," I said jokingly.

"Nope," Ben Lee said, "You want my long dong, but that ain't on the menu."

"Right," I said, "I deserved that one."

"You do," he said and went through the kitchen door.

A few minutes later Me Ly came with my food. The smell was incredibly intoxicating. The aroma of good curry can open up your sinuses like nothing else on earth.

"I am sorry I upset you," I told Me Ly as she was putting down my food, "I was only joking with you."

"That is OK," Me Ly said with a perfectly serene face. "I can get, how do you say it, a... accustomed to you. A dog can get accustomed to his fleas and so, I can get accustomed to you." Then she turned to walk to the kitchen.

"I'd like to be your flea," I said just barely loud enough for her to hear and she glanced over her shoulder and smiled.

I drank a Tsingtao with my beef curry and chicken fried rice. The beer was cold and smooth and good. The taste of the food was incredible. While I ate and drank, I was in heaven.

When I was almost finished with my meal, I took out the photo of Felicia playing chess. I looked at it for a while and thought about what she had written in her diary. I knew where I had to go next.

I put Felicia's photo away and finished my meal. I took my last swallow of Tsingtao, good stuff, and stood up.

Me Ly came out of the kitchen heading for another part of the restaurant. Our eyes met. She smiled shyly. Damn she looked sweet. I left her a large tip.

Yeah, I said to myself, as I walked to the door and watched Me Ly's butt as she walked to a customer's table, I sure would like to have slop chewy tonight.

Then I walked through the door and out into the street.

CHAPTER 14
SCHOOL DAYS

It wasn't raining yet today but the clouds were heavy and the sky looked like it was ready to start crying at any moment. I drove over to Felicia's high school, South Central, and went to the reception desk.

The receptionist was a young bright eyed black woman in her late twenties or early thirties. She looked like the type who would be the perfect straight laced librarian who would forever be sneaking into the adult section to peek at the forbidden knowledge. I bet I could teach her a few things she'd never learn from the textbooks in this school.

She smiled at me and came over to where I leaned on the counter. "May I help you in any way?" she asked.

I knew how she could help me, but instead I said, "I need to talk to the guy who organizes this school's chess club."

"Well, that would be Coach Wilson," she said and smiled again. She had one of those big African mouths with big African lips. I knew what that mouth was made for.

She looked at her watch and said, "He's between classes right now. I'll just buzz him on the PA."

"Tell him I'm here about Felicia Richardson," I told the receptionist.

A minute or two later, she told me Coach Wilson would meet me in the hall just outside the reception office.

She smiled at me again with that big mouth and the flash of white told me she had some big teeth to go along with those big lips. She'd have to be careful with those choppers or she'd have some Romeo crying for mercy.

In less than five minutes the coach showed up.

The coach looked like he was an ex-football player. Donald Wilson was about six foot three and he carried somewhere around two hundred and forty solid pounds and, he was white. The very fact that he was a white gym coach in a nearly all black school told me that this guy had to be one tough dog.

The coach gave my hand a strong shake and asked me what he could do for me.

"Do you remember a student you have on your chess team, Felicia Richardson?"

He nodded yes.

"I've been hired to try to locate her," I said. "The chess club seems to be a large part of her life and I was wondering if you'd seen anyone around her recently who you'd never seen before."

"You mean like someone who just doesn't seem to belong on the chess tournament scene," he asked.

"Yeah," I said. "I believe she was kidnapped and I'm looking for someone I believe was following her. But I have no name and no real description as of yet."

The coach rubbed his chin. He looked at the floor and forward while thinking. After a few moments he said, "I do try to pick up on people who hang around the kids and who don't seem to have much interest in competitive chess. The problem is that these chess tournaments are open to the public, so anyone can walk in and we do have a lot of people who show up just to watch what's going on."

"Did you notice anyone," I asked, "Who seemed to be watching Felicia in particular?"

"This is strange," Coach Wilson said. "Like I just said, I try to pick up on guys who hang around the kids and there was this one guy who I noticed was coming to tournaments a lot. Whether he was watching Felicia in particular, I'm not sure. But it seemed like every time I went to go ask him who he was, he would be gone. It was weird, almost like he would vanish right in front of me. So I never got a chance to ask him who he was."

"Do you remember what he looked like," I asked.

"Well, let's see," the coach said. "Judging him against my own size, which is the only way I can do it, and taking into consideration that I never got very close to him, I may be off some. Well, I have to say he was around six one or six two."

"His build?" I asked.

63

"Well, he was slim. I'd have to guess he weighs around two hundred pounds. Another thing, this guy always had on a nice black three-piece suit. That might have been why I noticed him. People are usually casual around these events."

"His skin color?" I asked.

"This guy was black," the coach said. "I mean really black, like charcoal."

I nodded. "Is there anything else you could tell me about this guy that made him stand out?"

"Well," the coach said. "That's the thing. He didn't stand out. I'm having to really search the bottom of my memory to give you what little I did. It's like I'm trying to remember a ghost. I just can't get a clear picture of what he looked like in my mind. I wish I could help you more."

"You've given me more than I had," I told him.

We shook hands again. A good firm handshake. Then Coach Wilson said, "I hope you find Felicia. She's a good kid. This was my first job teaching after I ruined my knees on a minor league baseball team. I only planned on staying here about two years until I could go to a better district. Kids like Felicia are the reason I'm still here after fifteen years. She has the kind of brains that she can be anything she'd want to be. But kids like her need good teachers to push them in the right direction."

"I'm sure you do that," I said.

"I try," he answered.

"And I'll try to get Felicia back home," I told him.

*   *   *

From the school, I walked to a corner 7-11 store and bought a small pad of paper and a pen. I figured it was about time I started keeping notes since my memory doesn't seem to be worth shit anymore. I might run across some information that, put with some other stuff, would tell me who this guy was who was following Felicia. But I knew if I don't write it down and try to remember it later, it will be gone like the wind.

In the car, I wrote down the description the coach had given me.

Black, real black like charcoal.

That matched Felicia's description.

The coach said he always had on a nice black three piece suit. Felicia said he dresses rich. On these two points, they match, so I figure it's the same guy.

OK! I'll put the coaches and Felicia's descriptions together.

I got: Coal black skin, penetrating eyes, dresses in suits, around thirty years old; around six feet one or six feet two, slim built around two hundred pounds.

Damn, I never even asked the coach what the guy's hair was like. But I guess I'd have to assume it was nothing unusual or else he would have noticed.

My description was real skimpy but at least it was better than nothing. Not much but a little better.

CHAPTER 15
THE PAST NEVER FORGETS

Back at my apartment, I turn the TV on. I turn it off. Not sure what I want to do. I want to dig up some facts to try and track down this guy but fuck, the truth is I ain't trained for this shit.

What the fuck, do I look like Nancy Drew? It pisses me off.

I feel like punching the wall. But hell, I'd just have to hang another picture to cover the hole. I got too many damn pictures on the wall as it is.

A knock on the door interrupts my self-ass whipping.

I answer the door and Julia is standing there in her hospital whites. She looks like a Hershey Chocolate Bar. Tasty, chewy, and juicy.

Damn, I think to myself, I'm getting as bad as Johnny. If I don't get fucked soon, fucking is going to be the only thing on my mind.

Without a word, I let Julia into the apartment.

"I just came by," she said. "To see if you'd learned anything from Felicia's diary."

"Well," I said, and walked over and picked up the diary, then gave it to Julia. "Felicia knew someone was following her."

"Who?" Julia asked.

"I don't have a name yet," I answered. "But I got some kind of idea as to what he looks like. Let's see if this rings a bell. He's around six foot one or two, around two hundred pounds, dresses real well, like in suits, and he's got real dark black skin like charcoal. You know anybody like this?" I ask.

"The truth is," Julia says. "The only men I know are the ones I work around. Doctors, orderlies, people like that, but I can't think of anybody who looks like what you said."

"Are you sure?" I ask her again.

"What," Julia says her voice rising. "Do you think for one minute if I thought I had any idea who had my little baby I'd hold that back. That's my baby," Julia almost screamed. "She's out there somewhere and I don't know what's being done to her. I want her home."

Tears almost came, but Julia fought them back.

I walked to the icebox and looked in. My supply was almost gone. I had to make a run to the liquor store soon.

This time I fish out a pint of Johnnie Walker Black Label whiskey. Take a drink of it and walk back to Julia.

I offer her a drink. She shakes her head no.

Julia sits on my couch. I sit beside her.

Quietly Julia says, "I need Felicia home. She's all that I've got."

I take a drink and listen.

"When Felicia's daddy was with me, I wasn't nothing but just one of those drugged out hoes that hang out on the streets all night. All we did was stay stoned all the time. Leroy, that was Felicia's daddy's name, Leroy Jones, used to rent me out to anybody who'd pay. When I got pregnant, he told me to get an abortion but I wouldn't do it. So about a month before Felicia was born, he left. I never knew where he went. I got locked up about a week after Felicia was born for marijuana possession. They took her away from me. It took me three years to get out of jail and get Felicia back.

"They only let me have her back because I got myself together and went through a nursing program. I proved I could handle being a good mother. Ever since then, it's only been me and Felicia. She's the reason I keep working and trying. I don't know what I'd do if I knew she was gone forever. I don't know if I'd even want to live," Julia whispered.

I totally understood how she felt. For a long time now I hadn't cared whether I lived or died. But my heart kept on beating anyway.

"You know," Julia said. "About five years ago, Leroy called me. Talking some shit about how he's the chosen one and how he wanted to see me and his baby. I told him he could go fuck himself. I didn't need him. Getting screwed over once by him was enough."

"That's the right attitude," I told Julia.

"It's the only one," she answered.

We sat on the couch in silence for a while. The silence was heavy with revealed secrets.

I picked up my pint bottle of Johnnie Walker. I took a long drink. I offered Julia a drink. She shook her head no again.

"You know," she said. "You could be a pretty nice guy. But why do you drink so much?"

I took another drink. Julia looked in my eyes. "You know," I say. "There are some things that are none of your fucking business."

"Well, I can accept that," Julia replied.

"You'll have to," I told her. "Nothing personal."

She stands up. "That's all right," she says.

"I'm going to keep working on this," I told Julia. "I'm going to get Felicia home to you."

I stand up and Julia looks in my eyes again, "I think you will," she says. "Or at least, I have to believe you will."

"I'm going to," I said as Julia was leaving.

It was as much a promise to myself as it was to her.

She opened the door and stepped out.

"Julia!" I called to her.

She stopped and looked back at me. Our eyes met.

I said, "There are some things I can't talk about."

"I understand," she said. "But if you ever need a good ear, come find me." Then she walked away.

Watching her walk down the hall I said to myself, "I just might." But the part of her I was watching walk was a bit lower than her ears.

I don't know why, but I felt real tense. Like there was some kind of electricity in the air and something crazy was just getting ready to let loose. So I went to the closet and got out a box of Thirty-Eight shells and loaded up my inside jacket pocket with about thirty of them.

Whatever was out there tonight, I was going to be ready.

CHAPTER 16
THE JAMAICAN BOY SCOUTS

At Johnny's I sit and brood over my Budweiser. Just trying to figure out what to do next to try and find this guy.

I'm not really paying attention to Johnny or the TV and we're the only two people in the bar.

"Dead assed day," Johnny says. "Not a goddamned person in here all day except for some damn drunk wandered in wantin me to give him a free beer. I told him I ain't your daddy and if I was I'd beat your ass for being a drunk."

I grunted into my beer and mumbled, "That's good customer relations."

"Better than he deserved," Johnny said.

I nodded and looked into the bubbles of my beer.

"What the fuck is wrong with you?" Johnny asked. "You look like someone fucked your cat or something."

"Just thinkin that's all," I said. "I want to find that little girl whose picture I showed you. But I'm not sure what the hell to do next."

"Well," Johnny said. "She sure ain't in that beer you've been staring at. And I tell you what, it's no secret that your main talent ain't thinkin. You just don't have the brain for it."

"So what hell do you suggest?" I ask Johnny.

"Relax man," Johnny said. "People like us, we're not methodical. If we need the answer to a complex problem our unconscious will help us out after a while. We just got to relax and let the inner computer do it."

I looked at Johnny and said, "That's a big help, Doctor Spock."

"Well, shit," Johnny says. "You ain't no goddamned genius."

We sat in silence for a while. Except when Johnny made a comment on the newswoman on KXOK who keeps bobbing her head up and down as she talks.

"Good neck motion," Johnny says slowly. "I taught her that one."

"Yeah right," I said. "And the fags at Chesney Park taught you."

"Fuck you," Johnny said and laughed.

"No thanks, not my type," I said.

"I know what you need," Johnny says.

"What's that?" I ask.

"You need your ass kicked in some chess. That'd bring you down a peg or two. Just where you white motherfuckers ought to be, below the black man."

"You think it'd cheer me up to whip the hell out of you again. Well, I guess I'll do it," I say.

"Naw man," Johnny said. "I ain't in the mood to be whippin your ass. But there's some guy been hanging around Roxie's tellin everyone he's never been beat. You can play him while I check out the titties."

Johnny has an enthusiastic smile on his face.

"Is that all you ever think about," I ask Johnny, "Titties?"

"Oh no, not at all," he says and gets up, goes behind the bar, and locks the cash register. "I think about all kinds of things, legs, thighs, butts, lips. I think about all kinds of things. All of them female."

We walk to the door.

"Your boyfriend is going to be jealous," I tell Johnny.

*   *   *

Johnny locks up his bar and I study the sky. The clouds are low and dark and ominous looking. Off to the east I can see flashes of light from lightning still in the clouds.

It hadn't yet started raining but a storm was definitely coming.

Distant rumbles shook the ground. It matched the way I felt tonight. On edge, tight, waiting for something to happen.

We walked around to the alley on the side of Johnny's Bar and Grill and got in his car. It was an old green Ford Maverick that had so much rust it looked like it was almost a form of camouflage.

"Why you drive this piece of shit?" I asked Johnny. "Hell, this thing looks worse than my car."

Johnny turned the motor over. The old car coughed once then purred smoothly.

"I tell ya why I like this car," Johnny said. "This here car is like a horrible lookin woman with a great heart that loves ya. That woman, she knows what to do and she's doin it for you. So if you're smart you'll learn to love her looks and enjoy what you got."

I look at Johnny and say, "So what the fuck does that have to do with cars."

"Well," he says, "About three years ago I got kind of tired of this car and leased me a new car. I kept this one and drove it every now and then but I was trying to kill it by mistreatment. Hell, I even drove it on diesel for a while. But it just smoked like hell and made some clacking noises and kept on goin just like it always had. But hell, that new car every time the weather changed, it didn't want to start. Something was always going wrong with that damn thing. Finally the motherfucker quit on me at a stop light right next to Laclede's Landing one night when I had a hot babe with me. The babe got mad cause I lost it and kicked the crap out of the car."

"So now I'm back to my baby." he leaned forward and kissed the steering wheel. "Never gonna stray again. Till she goes to that junkyard in the sky."

"You make a good couple," I told Johnny as he pulled out of the alley.

"Damn right we do," he said.

"But ain't she gonna be jealous tonight?" I asked.

"Only if we go see some naked cars," Johnny said.

We cruised toward Washington Park where Roxie's was, past the closed down buildings, the drunks, the bums and the prostitutes. We cruised down Fourth Street slowly, almost like sightseers watching the show.

We cruised past the Barbary Coast Tavern and my heart skipped a beat. It was almost dark and at the same spot, beside the Barbary Coast Tavern where I had spotted him the same night I'd killed him, was Morris West.

I blinked and shook my head.

Johnny saw me and said, "Looks a lot like him, don't it?"

On second look, I did see it wasn't Morris West. But someone who did look a hell of a lot like him. He had the same dread lock Jamaican look

71

about him, the same head to toe black clothes and the same kind of sunglasses worn after dark. But this guy was slightly shorter.

It was a different guy, even if he did shop at the same stores that Morris did.

"I'd have to figure," Johnny said. "That spot is kind of like a franchise. Like McDonalds. If someone offs the manager of Mickey D's the next one there is gonna have the same boss and he's gonna wear the same uniform."

I said, "Kind of like the Jamaican boy scouts, right?"

"Yeah, except these ones sell poison," Johnny said and drove on.

CHAPTER 17
T & A BREAK

Great big heavy raindrops started hitting the car's windshield and roof just before we saw the neon sign of Roxie's. They sounded like rocks being thrown against the car.

The downpour that the clouds had long promised was finally arriving. It was eleven o'clock, dark, and stormy.

Roxie's sign appeared around the turn. It was a big neon with the name Roxie's above the neon outline of a woman hiking her skirt up.

Johnny drove around back of the building, then came out to the front through an alley beside Roxie's. He parked in the alley with the front end of the car sticking out of the darkness between Roxie's and an abandoned building next door.

Johnny shut the engine off. He looked at me with a very serious look on his face and yelled, "Titties!!!" Then laughed real loud.

"Man, you almost made me jump out of my socks," I told Johnny.

He laughed some more. "Come on," he said and we both got out of the car and went inside.

The guy at the door, a big black weight lifter type, charged us each a five dollar cover charge. I paid for me and Johnny.

"Thanks brother," he said.

"That's all right," I told him, "You're getting the first round of drinks."

Strobes were flashing above three raised platforms where three women danced to the pulsing rhythms of sleazy strip music. The music was some of that shit they call new wave. Hell, shit music is shit music no matter what you call it. They call it new wave. I call it new shit. It still stinks.

We walked into the place toward the bar. Johnny's eyes were like saucers trying to devour all of the bare skin that he could see. And there was a lot of it to see.

The customers sat at chairs around the platforms and fished for dollars to stick in the girls' G-strings when it was their turn to do so. I have never seen the logic of doing that. Whether you give the women any money or not doesn't make any difference. You're not going to get fucked by them by giving them money. They expect that from all the guys.

There were several tables in the middle of the room with guys drinking and talking at them. At some of the tables, semi-naked girls sat with the guys. I knew the girls were sipping high priced drinks that they made a high commission off of.

At one table there was a black man and a white guy playing chess. I figured one of them was going to be my opponent in a while.

We were almost to the bar when a cute little brunette came up to us and asked, "Is there anything I can do for you?" She smiled wickedly and looked in my eyes, then her gaze slid down my body, stopped at my crotch, then slid back up again to my eyes.

I felt like a soup bone being eyed by a pit bull dog. But I will admit, looking at her tight little body in the tight tee shirt and bikini panties did make my dick twitch.

"Yeah," Johnny said. "Lots a thing you can do. Right now, I'll take me a JD and coke."

"And what would be your pleasure?" She asked me, smiling that wicked smile.

I couldn't help but smile back even though I knew her flirting was only an act.

"I'll take a Royal Crown and Seven," I told her and she went for the drinks.

I could feel the thumping of the music in my bones and the place smelled like a combination of sweat, smoke and cheap perfume.

We went to a table near one of the platforms where a chic with obviously dyed red hair twirled around making her hair look like a red feather duster. She was trying to dance like a ballerina, but she was carrying about seventy pounds too much to be able to dance with any grace at all, no matter what style she chose. The way she jiggled around the stage made me wonder if she wrote on her dance resume the description, "Remember Jell-O Pudding goes with everything."

Johnny jumped up, "I gotta get a closer look at that," he told me and went to the stage.

Me-- hell, I couldn't get far enough away.

The fake red head bent over in front of a customer and spread her enormous cheeks for him to get a wide open view.

Jesus, I thought, I hope she ain't had no chili today. If she lets it fly right now, she'll take that poor guy's head off.

I turned away from that chamber of horrors and looked at the chess players.

The white guy was studying the board intently. He looked like he was trying to see the floor right through the board and table. I guess he was trying to develop x-ray vision or something like it. He had a short haircut and wore a jean jacket with a Harley Davidson symbol on it.

The black guy was smiling like he knew the location of buried treasure and was just about to dig it up. He was wearing a white shirt rolled up at the sleeves and had a black jacket over the back of his chair. He was laughing under his breath. I was guessing he was doing it to unnerve his opponent.

I stood up to go to the bar and when I turned, I bumped into the brunette who was bringing the drinks.

"Oh," she said. "You can bump into me anytime." She wore her ever perpetual wicked smile.

I took the drinks and sat them on the table. I motioned at Johnny who had his neck craned to the side and was looking right into the pit of hell between that fat dancers twin, beach ball, ass cheeks.

"He's paying for these," I told the brunette.

She pursed her lips at me like her feelings were hurt, "Can't you give little Dallas a tip?" She asked with a whine.

I gave her a dollar.

Dallas took the dollar and looked at it in her hand disdainfully. "Can't you give Dallas a better tip than that?" She smiled imitating a little girl's pout.

"Yeah," I said stepping around her. "Get your ass back to school and get out of this shit."

I went to the bar.

Sammy Jones, a tall fat black guy, was tending bar.

"What's the hap, John?" He said and we slapped palms over the bar. I hadn't seen Sammy for a couple of months but we were old buddies. We used to run around together when we were teenagers about a thousand years ago.

I took the photo of Felicia playing chess out of my pocket and showed it to him.

"I'm trying to find this kid," I told Sammy. "She's missing."

Sammy looked at the picture.

"Is she a good, clean kid?" He asked.

"Yeah," I answered.

"You won't find her in here," Sammy said.

"I know," I said taking the picture back from his big hands, "Just asking around."

I looked around the room and Johnny was at the second stage. A blond dancer was kneeling down in front of him. He was rubbing on her legs and saying something to her while putting dollars in her G-string. I didn't know what Johnny was saying but it's a sure bet he wasn't talking about bible school. The dancer was built all right but her face looked like it had worn out three bodies.

Sammy slapped me on the shoulder.

"We need to put a leash on Johnny," he said with a short laugh.

"Hell," I said. "He's just gettin started."

CHAPTER 18
DIVINE CANDI

On the third stage, Candi Divine was dancing. I'd heard of that dancer. With long muscular legs, large breasts, deep chocolate skin, and a face like an African goddess, this dancer had all the equipment men would dream about and something extra. For some strange reason there were no guys at that stage giving Candi any dollars.

Most of the guys were only brave enough to give Candi Divine curious looks from across the room. Candi Divine was the kind of woman that scared the hell out of most guys. Me included.

I showed a couple more people around the bar Felicia's photo and all I got were head shakes and sorrys. I headed back to our table.

Johnny came back to the table mimicking wiping sweat from his forehead.

"Woo, that's some hot pussy," he said, acting like he was flinging sweat to the floor from his hand. With these sleazy chicks, Johnny was in heaven.

At the chess player's table, the black guy got up to go and got a drink. He was tall and very dark. A waitress met him before he was halfway to the bar. He expressed himself with big expansive hand gestures when he talked.

It was like he was trying to cast some kind of magic spell. He must have thought he was the coolest guy on earth. He went back to his table.

I asked Johnny, "Which of those guys am I supposed to play?"

He said, "Tor Ambrose, the black guy. He's a sorry-assed dog, son-of-a-bitch, but he plays a hell of a game of chess.

"Well," I said. "I won't feel so bad about beating his ass. Since he's such a dog."

"No shit," Johnny said. "He is damn good. He knows it too. He likes to talk shit while he plays. When we played, he actually told me he was chosen to have powers others of us don't have."

"Sounds like he's full of shit," I told Johnny.

"Yeah," Johnny said. "He wasn't too happy when I told him he only had the power to suck my dick and to shut up."

"He looks like he's your type," I said.

"Man," Johnny said. "You need to stop with that shit."

"OK," I said, "I'll chill out."

"Anyway," Johnny said. "Tor thinks he knows voodoo or some shit like that. So watch him, he might try to put the evil eye on ya or something. My Grandma from Louisiana taught me all about that shit."

"Do you believe in that shit?" I asked Johnny.

"Naw man," he said. "I'm a modern type guy but my Grandma was always tellin me about it. So I know about it anyway."

Two dancers left their stages and were replaced by two new ones. Candi Divine stayed where she was dancing.

Evidently Candi wasn't ready to quit dancing yet and there wasn't anyone big enough to tell her that her turn was up.

The song *Kung Fu Fighting* started playing and on the first stage an Oriental woman introduced as Sushi started dancing. If I would have been sitting at the stage, I would have backed up.

Sushi was doing an imitation of a Kung Fu fight and was flinging herself all over the place while throwing punches and kicks. It looked like she could come flying off of there at any moment and knock the crap out of one of the customers.

At the chess players' table the white guy slapped the tabletop then both of the players stood up. Tor laughed out a loud mocking laugh and the other guy left pissed off.

On the stage, Sushi was in the middle of throwing a whirlwind of kicks and punches. She was short and kind of skinny but I wouldn't want to get her pissed off.

"Looks like it's my turn," I told Johnny motioning to the table where Tor Ambrose sat.

I got up.

"Good luck," Johnny said. "Kick his ass."

"Lucks got nothing to do with it," I said and went over to where Tor was receiving his drink from the waitress and was resetting the pieces.

Our eyes met.

"They tell me you say you've never been beat," I tell him.

He laughs. It was that cola nut guy laugh. The same kind of laugh that the guy in the Seven-Up commercial uses.

"It is not only what I say," Tor says. "But that is how it is. I have never been beat."

"Then get ready for a new experience," I told him and sat down.

We flipped for colors and he won white.

He moved his King's Pawn forward two squares.

"I am Tor Ambrose," he told me. I felt his eyes boring into my head. He had been staring at me non-stop since I came over here.

"I know who you are," I told him. "Now are you my bitch or what?"

"What?" he asked.

"If you ain't my bitch," I told Tor. "Then quit looking at me like you want me to fuck you."

I moved my King's Pawn forward two squares.

He laughed again but his eyes did shift away.

"You are a funny man," he said and I noticed he spoke with a deep Caribbean accent.

Johnny was over at Sushi's stage now. He was standing in front of her doing karate poses. Sushi had a big grin on her face. If Johnny had his way, he'd be showing Sushi his lethal technique of Tongue Fu.

Tor moved his Queen's Knight in front of his Bishop's Pawn.

He smiled and looked at me intently trying to read my face expression.

"There you are," I told him, meeting his gaze. "Acting like my bitch again."

The smile left his face.

I moved my Queen's Bishop Pawn forward one square.

Tor's lips curled back into a sneer.

"I'm tired of your jokes," he snarled.

Tor moved his King Bishop's Pawn forward two squares.

"I don't give a fuck what you like," I told him and moved my black square Bishop diagonally three squares so it was three squares in front of my other Bishop.

"And there ain't shit you can do about anything I say or do."

Tor looked like he was going to jump up out of his chair and attack me. He was so pissed off his eyes were bulging out of his head and the veins on his neck stood out.

"Go ahead," I told him. "I ain't liked you since the first minute I saw you." I put my right hand inside my jacket right where my gun was holstered and curled my fingers around the grip of my Thirty-Eight.

"You're like shit with perfume poured on it," I said, our eyes locked. "The fine clothes, the smooth talk might fool some people, but I know what you are. Just shit."

Someone pulled my hat off and I jerk to the side and see Dallas rubbing my hat on her breasts. "Oooh," she said, "Your head is warm. You need to cool off." She laughed and put my hat back on me.

I smiled at her then look back at Tor.

"Move, Tar baby," I tell him.

Tor smiled slyly then captures my Pawn with his King Bishop's Pawn.

"It matters not what you do tonight," Tor said studying the board. "I will come for you tomorrow. For at midnight, I drink the blood of the lamb and I will gain more power than you can imagine exists."

"Yeah, I heard you think you're some kind of voodoo Joe or something," I told Tor. "Well, talk that shit to someone else."

Dallas leaned close to my ear and whispered, "Are you really a Private Detective? I always thought those guys were so cool." Her breathing sounded like she had just run a mile, uphill all the way.

Just another dizzy chic, I thought. Well, nobody comes here for intellectual enlightenment now do they?

"Yeah," I told her, "That's what I do. I detect all the girl's privates."

Dallas giggled a dizzy little girl's giggle and leaned close again. "I'll be back," she breathed into my ear. She pranced away trying to look perky.

Tor moved and I immediately moved. I was looking around the room hardly looking at the board when I did move.

What I was trying to do was make Tor think that I held him in so much contempt that I wasn't even paying attention. In reality, I was watching the board very closely. I was making plans and was preparing to execute. I just wanted Tor to think he was playing an idiot who didn't care if he won or lost.

I hadn't been lying when I'd told Tor that I couldn't stand him at first sight. I didn't know what, but something about his guy just reeked.

Johnny came up to the table. He pulled up a chair and sat down.

Tor gave him a mean look. "Can you not see I am trying to concentrate," he told Johnny.

"You look like you're trying to take a shit," Johnny said and we slap palms.

"Damn," Johnny said. "All this hot pussy here, gettin me hornier that a motherfucker. I'm gonna have to fuck me something tonight."

Tor moved again and I immediately move again. I was thinking, I did have him rattled. He looked like he was trying to see something happening on the board that wasn't actually there.

"I tell you what," I said to Johnny. "I've been seeing a dancer watching you all night. Everywhere you go she's got her eyes on you."

"You're full of shit," Johnny said.

"No man, I ain't bullshittin," I told him. "Hell, you're a good lookin guy. If I was a bitch, I'd fuck you myself." I put my hand on Johnny's leg and he slapped it off.

"Back up Jack," he said.

"I was almost overwhelmed," I told Johnny and laughed.

Tor interrupted us. "We have a game to play," he said through tight lips.

"I'll get to you, Mogombo," I told Tor.

Tor was seething in menacing silence. He was breathing heavy again and almost shaking in fury.

Johnny looked at me and said, "John, you really should take it easy on the spook."

We both laughed and slapped palms.

I point at Candi Divine who is still on the stage and tell Johnny, "That's the one that wants you."

CHAPTER 19
DOGGIN' DALLAS

The moment that I pointed at Candi Divine, Johnny and Candi locked eyes.

Candi had been doing some body building poses when it happened. The music that Candi was flexing to was *Body Language* by Queen. Candi's whole body writhed and Candi looked oddly like a tensing boa constrictor.

Tor looked from me to Johnny and said, "You are both going to die."

"No shit," Johnny said absently, with his eyes still locked to Candi's. He pushed his chair back and got up. He said, "I think I'll make my death by fucking." Johnny walked to where Candi was.

He's got more guts than I have, I thought as I watched him approach Candi. Within two minutes they were at a table making goo-goo eyes at each other. Boy was Johnny in for a surprise.

Tor moves again and I move again instantly and see a plan developing. I'm going to sacrifice my Knight and within three moves, he'll have to give me his Queen or be checkmated.

I watch as Johnny leads Candi to the dance floor and they start slow dancing. I take the photo of Felicia playing chess out of my pocket and sit it down beside the chessboard facing Tor.

"Have you seen this girl?" I ask him.

Tor's eyes flash to the picture, then his eyes flash back up to mine filled with rage.

He says, "I am tired of your children's games. You are trying to distract me. It is the only way you could ever hope to win."

Tor stands up and I stand up.

"Well, make your move bad boy," I tell him. "I want to bust you upside your head so bad I can taste it."

At that moment Johnny yells from the dance floor, "What the fuck is this?"

He pushes Candi away from him.

"Jesus." Johnny yells. "You got a dick bigger than I do."

Candi has her hands on her hips and her head rocking side to side. At that moment she, or he, was a big beautiful muscular African Amazon Queen and he, or she, was as scary as hell.

"That's right," Candi barked at Johnny with her head rocking. "I'm more woman than you can ever handle and more man than you'll ever be."

"Fuck this," Johnny yelled and came stomping back to the table.

I couldn't help but grin.

"And you think this is funny," he said to me. "Fuck you too!"

Johnny bumps into the table and some chess pieces fall over.

"You stupid idiot," Tor yells.

"That's redundant dummy," I yell back at Tor.

"That's telling him," Johnny says.

Someone has curled their fingers around my arms and was turning me to face them. I turned and saw Dallas looking up at me with wide eyes and pouty lips.

"Mr. Detective man," she slid her hands down my arm, grabbed my hand, and started pulling me across the floor. "You big sexy Mr. Detective man," she said exaggerating each word, each word flowing off her tongue like liquid. "I need you to investigate something." She led me across the floor then pulled me through the door to the dressing rooms. "Oooh yeah," Dallas cooed as she pulled me down a short hall to a room where a piece of paper tacked to a door identified the dressing room as being hers.

"I need to investigate you too," she said breathlessly and pulled me through the door and latched it behind me.

Dallas unzipped my fly and pulled my dick out. "Oh what a big boy," she breathed as she stroked me hard. Then she went down on her knees and made my dick disappear between her parted lips. She sucked me hard making wet squishing noises as her head went forward and back from my crotch.

With a smack of her lips, Dallas pulled her face away from my dick, stood up, and turned her back to me. With one motion, she bent over, dropped her panties to the floor and kicked them away from her.

"Oooh," she said. "I need an in-depth probe. You got to fuck me from behind. You need to investigate me."

This dizzy chic was really getting into this detective stuff. But what the hell, I could play along.

"All right doll face," I told her. "I'll get to the root of the problem."

I got behind her. She stuck her ass in the air and I slid all the way into her. I lost my balance and we both pushed forward. Dallas's head rammed into the wall.

"Oh God," she panted.

I went to pull her away from the wall as she grabbed my legs and pulled me deep into her again and banged her head against the wall again.

"Oh God, I love it," she wailed. "It makes me see stars."

This chic really does want her brains fucked out, I thought.

"Oh God, bang me through the wall," Dallas yelled.

So I tried to do exactly that. I was slamming into her from behind and her head was slamming into the wall. Thank God I don't have to talk to this chic later, I thought. She probably won't have enough brains left to say shit.

I was banging her against the wall so much that at first I didn't hear that banging that was coming through the door. I could hear yelling too. It was Johnny.

"Open the door," he was yelling, "Open the door." And he kept beating on the door.

"Shut the fuck up," I yelled at Johnny and I swear to God, I didn't even miss a stroke.

Dallas was Oohing and Aaaawing and Johnny was banging on the door so much that I had a hard time getting my nut. But like the hardworking man that I am, I kept at it until I did cum. And I made damn sure I pulled out just before I came and shot my cum all over Dallas's ass.

No way in hell did I want to take the chance of having any rug rat with this dizzy chic. The world has enough problems right now without that.

I zipped myself up, blew Dallas a kiss, and went out into the hallway where Johnny waited.

CHAPTER 20
TOR AMBROSE

What the fuck is wrong with you?" I asked Johnny. "Couldn't you tell I was on the job in there?"

Back here where the music was muffled, I could hear the rain beating down on the roof. It must be pouring buckets down outside, I thought.

"I know who's got your little girl," Johnny says.

"What are you talking about?" I asked.

"The instant you left the table Tor picked up the picture," Johnny showed me the photo of Felicia playing chess that I had left on the table. "He threw it back down and told me he's going to kill us all and he slapped the chess pieces over."

"I told him, he ain't gonna kill shit and that was a forfeit so he stomped his ass out the front door. I picked up the picture and looked at it and look!" Johnny pointed to a figure in the background. Even though he was blurred, the figure was Tor.

It hit me then all at once. Tor fit the description I had worked up to a tee. I had been sitting there staring at him all night and hadn't even realized it. Tor was tall, thin, had coal black skin, penetrating eyes, looked to be around thirty, wore really nice clothes, and he definitely had the attitude to refer to himself as the King in cheesy poetry to a little girl.

I could of kicked the crap out of myself for being so stupid. And something else hit me too.

"You know about voodoo, right?" I asked Johnny.

"Yeah, some," he said.

"Well, what does it mean if you say you're going to drink the blood of the lamb at midnight and gain great power?" I asked.

"If Tor told you that," Johnny said. "Then he's going to sacrifice an innocent child at midnight to a dark God so he gains some kind of magical powers."

I looked at my watch. It read nine thirty.

I looked at Johnny, "I got two and a half hours to find this bastard and stop him from killing Felicia."

"We have two and a half hours!" Johnny said. "I know who this guy is and how to find him and I ain't letting you do this by yourself."

PART III

END GAME!

Go ahead punk,
Make my day!
- Dirty Harry

Sometimes the good guys
And the bad guys
Both
Wear Black Hats
- The Walker in Darkness

Mercy ain't
A part of the Game
- Sonny Liston

CHAPTER 21
BLACK BLADE IN THE NIGHT

While we were walking out of the dressing rooms hallway, Johnny told me that Tor was the supplier of these Jamaican dealers that had been around the area for about eight months now. He knew this because Tor offered him money to be able to sell crack out of his bar.

Johnny told him to leave or die and that ended that conversation.

"All we got to do to find Tor," Johnny told me. "Let's go make his dealer at the Barbary Coast tell us where he lives. That's where Tor would do any sacrificing too. These voodoo people cast spells in their homes. That's where their center of power always is."

"OK," I told Johnny as we passed through the door and back into the nightclub. "We go get that dealer right now and he will tell us where Tor's home is or I'll cut his fingers and toes off one by one."

A table of drunken guys cheered me when they saw me emerge from the dressing room area.

I checked my fly. It was up. As I passed their table I gave them a victory salute with an upraised fist and told them, "It was a dirty job, but somebody had to do it."

We walked across the floor to the sound of their raucous laughter.

About halfway across the room Johnny told me, "You know man that was pretty fucking sorry what you pulled on me with Candi Divine."

"Yeah," I told him. "But you got to admit, it was pretty damn funny."

"Well, tomorrow I might laugh," he said. "But tonight I'm kinda pissed off. Hell, I've felt funny before, but that was the first time I've ever felt nuts, if you know what I mean."

"Yeah, I know what you mean," I said.

"Pay backs a bitch," Johnny said. "I'm gonna get you back for this one."

"Be my guest," I told him as we went out the front door, "If you can do it."

*　　*　　*

The rain came down in torrents. We were both soaked to the bone before we even made it to the car. Then Johnny had me standing there in the pouring rain while he fiddled around for the right key to open the door. I was wondering if he had about a hundred keys on that ring when he finally popped his door open.

When we were both inside but far from dry Johnny turned to me and asked, "You got your gun on ya?"

"Yeah," I told him. "I always do."

"I gotta get my baby," Johnny said and got out and went toward the blackness of the alley to the trunk of the car.

There was a bump against the car like Johnny had slipped and fallen onto the trunk. Then I heard Johnny shout a stream of obscenities and I came out of my door into the blinding rain drawing my thirty-eight.

At the rear of the car Johnny was on the ground on his back. He was shouting defiantly at a dark figure that stood over him.

I saw the knife in the figure's hand, a long gleaming black blade. I saw him reverse his grip from a slashing grip to a stabbing grip.

"Tor," I yelled and the figure froze and the face turned towards me. His eyes blazed into my eyes with purest evil hate.

I squeezed the trigger of my thirty-eight twice and sent two shots blasting into Tor's chest. The shots jerked him like he had been punched twice in the chest and he staggered back three steps. Then his feet went out from under him and he fairly flew off the cement and landed with a splash in a puddle on the pavement. The soles of his shoes went up into the air then came back down and he lay there.

I went to where Johnny lay and knelt down by him. He was wiping the rain out of his eyes.

"The bastard cut me," Johnny yelled.

"How bad is it?" I asked him and I could see his shirt sliced open over his chest in a long straight line.

"I'm bleeding like a bitch on her worst day but I'll live," he answered.

Mocking deep laughter came to me through the rain from out of the darkness. I looked up and saw Tor on his feet.

"You can't kill me," his voice thundered at me.

I took aim and my .38 roared three more times till I was pulling the trigger and clicking on empty chambers.

Each shot knocked Tor back like they were mule kicks. He staggered backwards into the darkness and I saw him no more.

I quickly reloaded the five chambers of my Undercover Special Thirty-Eight. The mocking laughter came again out of the darkness.

"You can't kill me!" Tor yelled again and his laughter receded away from us, and then was gone altogether.

People were coming out of Roxie's now drawn by the gunshots. I walked back into the darkness of the alley and saw how Tor had vanished so quickly. There was a manhole cover that was half slid off of the hole. I knew he went down there.

When I went back to Johnny, Sushi was there. She had Johnny's head on her lap and she was stroking his forehead.

A crowd was gathered now around Roxie's entrance and I yelled for one of them to call an ambulance. One of the dancers said she would and went back inside.

Sushi kissed Johnny on the forehead and wailed, "Oh Johnny, please, please don't die. I like you so much." She bawled. "Your head is like one big beautiful raisin," she told him.

"If you stay with me" Johnny told Sushi. "I might just pull through."

After hearing that line of bullshit, I knew Johnny was gonna be just fine.

Johnny fished his car keys out of his pocket and held them out to me. He tried to sit up and said, "Damn that fucking hurt." And relaxed back down against Sushi's legs.

I took his car keys.

"Get my sawed off double barrel twelve gauge out of the trunk," Johnny said. "Tor might laugh at your little pea shooter but that motherfucker will get his attention."

I got the gun and some shells that were scattered on the floor of the trunk and put them in my pants pocket.

Johnny held his hand up to me and I gripped it. "Do me a favor," Johnny said.

"What's that?" I asked.

"Blow that sorry bastards head off," he said, "And get that little girl home to her mother."

"Definitely," I said. Then I went down into the underworld.

CHAPTER 22
DOWN IN THE DARK

When I slid the manhole cover completely off the hole, it made a low metallic scraping noise. It was heavy as hell and I realized either Tor was an incredibly strong man to be able to move it as fast as he would have had to, or he set up his escape before he attacked. Either way I didn't like it.

If Tor was incredibly strong then he'd be a dangerous opponent in a hand to hand fight. If he'd planned ahead, Tor would be dangerous in any kind of a confrontation. Now I was entering a world that Tor was far more familiar with than I was.

I had never been down in the sewers beneath East St. Louis. But I was betting that Tor knew these tunnels very well. Even though I'd never admit it to him, I would have felt a lot better if Johnny was going to be with me going down into this hole.

The rain was pouring down and I could barely see as it was, and here I was going down into a pitch black hole with one hand carrying a shot gun and only one hand to hold the steel ladder with. If Tor decided to just wait at the bottom and get me as I came down, I'd be a sitting duck. I couldn't do anything to stop him from stabbing me in the leg, ass, or back, as I came down.

I tried to peer down into the blackness below to see how far down the bottom was. That was no good. All I saw was the swirling dark. The cement floor could be six or sixty feet below me for all I knew.

Time was ticking. I couldn't stop the clock, so I went down the ladder one rung at a time.

The ladder was wet, cold steel. It was slimy and slick as hell. I went down the ladder as quickly as I could but that was painfully slow.

I could see nothing below me. The only thing that I could see was the dim circle of light from above. I climbed down and my heart beat wildly. I tried to crane my head around to see behind me. With my one handed grip I could see nothing at all. At any second I expected to feel that long blade that Tor slashed Johnny with bite into my back.

I continued down one rung at a time. Then my left foot reached down for the next rung and it found only space. I looked down and saw only blackness.

What was it, two feet down to the cement or two hundred? Was the ladder just missing a few rungs and then went on for about twenty feet down? I didn't know.

Tor did know this way out. Of that I was sure. How else had he been able to go down the ladder that quickly?

Maybe he can see in the dark, the thought came to me. Well, maybe. The way he shrugged off those bullets I'd hit him with was downright unnerving. He thinks he can do voodoo. Shit maybe he can.

I couldn't stay there all night on the ladder wondering. If I wasted too much time, Felicia wouldn't live the night out.

So I stepped off the ladder and let myself fall straight down.

My stomach jumped as I went into free fall through the air. I fell about two feet.

I landed on some sort of iron grating that must of been covering a central drain way. I could hear water flowing below the iron grill I was standing on. For a moment I stood there listening, trying to hear anything that might point me in the direction that Tor had gone in.

I heard water dripping and trickling down the walls. From what seemed to be a great distance, I heard the slapping sound of what sounded like running.

I stepped out of my ring of diffused light that leaked down from above and found myself staring into complete and utter blackness. I stuck my left hand out and felt for the wall and found it.

The wall was slimy and cold but it would serve as some sort of guide to at least keep me from running headlong into another wall in the darkness.

As I moved along, I started to see vague shapes and outlines. I realized that I was starting to see a little bit. My eyes were beginning to adjust to the near total absence of light because I could see where small rays of light filtered down from above through other manholes and drainage grates.

I moved in the direction where I heard the sounds of running trying to increase my pace but being very aware of just how blind I was down here.

When I held out the shotgun in my right hand in front of my face, I could only see the dim outline of its three foot long length. If I tried to see the metal grate beneath my feet that I was walking on, I could see only black nothingness. I was only praying that there were no missing sections of grate or anything sitting up on top of the grate that I might trip over.

If I was to break my ankle or break my leg right now, then Felicia was dead. That was certain.

The sounds in front of me were increasing.

I could hear more of the slapping noises but now it didn't sound like running. There was no rhythm to the sound. There'd be a whack-whack then silence for a few seconds. Then another whack-whack.

I could hear low whispering voices and shuffling sounds.

I was moving towards these sounds but I wasn't sure anymore if Tor was making them. There seemed to be more than one voice up a head.

The illumination in the corridor up a head, about a half block away, was a lot brighter than where I was now. Smells came to me that were different from the ones I first smelled when coming down here.

Which was mustiness, rot, and the stale smell of shit and piss. Now I smelled something else. It was like the smell at a barbecue before you've added any sauce or spices to the meat. It was the smell of burning wood and burning flesh.

The light I saw, as I drew closer to it, was coming from a side channel corridor. It was uneven and flickering. I figured it must be some sort of campfire. I'd heard that there were some hobos living down here but of course I'd never come down here and seen them for myself.

This isn't exactly the kind of place you come to just hang out and have fun.

I edged up closely to the entranceway where the light was issuing out of and peered around the corner. After a short tunnel the entrance opened up into a large chamber.

There was a group of men hunched around a fire in the center of the chamber. The firelight showed that there was a domed roof and lines of the grates led to the center where the fire was built. Above ground this must be some kind of major intersection. Down here it was an intersection of drains and it looked like the picnic area for this group of bums.

I walked toward the group around the fire and no one even saw me coming. They were so intent upon the feast they were cooking that no one even looked up. The whack-whack sound that I heard I saw now was made by a short stump of a guy who was whacking with a hatchet on what looked like a side of beef laying on the cement.

I walked right up to the group, cleared my throat and said, "Has any of you seen someone come running through here?"

The whacking stopped. The mumbling and grumbling the others were doing stopped.

They all froze.

I froze.

All of them, I think there was around ten of them, stood up as one and turned toward me.

With them standing I saw between them what was on a spit turning over the fire.

It was a human leg.

They charged me. All of them at once. The ones on the far side of the fire leaped over it and came after me.

I belted the first one with the sawed off shot gun and kicked the second one in the nuts. Then they were on me. The whole pack bore me backwards and I was slammed into a cement wall by the sheer force of their superior weight and number.

I punched with my left and swung the Twelve Gauge like a club. Their fists struck at me. Their hands tore at me. There were too many arms and fists for me to block them all so I just absorbed a lot of blows as well as I could and struck back however I could with fists or feet or steel.

The mob that was on me stank to high heaven. I'd have to bet that none of them had taken a bath in a year. Add to that the fact that the breath of all of them seemed to smell like rotten meat and I was gagging each time I took a breath.

I was sliding along the wall with my back to it trying to beat them off me as well as I could when suddenly the wall was gone. I went flying backward into space and crashed to my back on some iron grating. On impact my head bounced hard off the steel under me and I saw points of light flash all around me.

He was looming above me. The stump of a man who I had seen hacking the chunks out of what I knew now was a human corpse.

He raised the hatchet in one hand and as I saw the sparks of my near unconsciousness dance around his head he bellowed, "He's mine!"

I don't know how I'd kept hold of the shotgun but I brought it up now.

I pulled the trigger and in a flash of roaring blindness my would-be butcher's head turned to a bowl of well sauced spaghetti that flew from his shoulders and splattered against the ceiling.

The others staggered back and I sent another shot into the spot where the group looked to be the tightest packed. Two more of these derelict cannibals went down screaming.

All of the rest scattered and ran for the openings to other tunnels.

One of them stumbled and went down. I ran to where he was trying to get up and stepped on his back to put him down on his face.

He was so terrified he could hardly talk and I wasn't in much of a talking mood myself. I knelt down on his back with my knees and jerked his head up by the hair.

"Where is he?" I yelled in his ear.

"I-I-I," he stammered in fright. "I don't know what you're talking about."

I wrenched his head up hard by the hair then let it fall back to the cement with a plop.

"If you don't tell me where the one who came before me went, I'll break your fucking neck!" I yelled.

"Over there, the ladder," he said and worked his arm out and pointed.

I saw the ladder and saw where it led up to the streets.

"OK," I told him and got up. "You did good."

Then I kicked him in the face as hard as I could.

"Tell that to your buddies next time you want to have someone for dinner," I told him, but I don't think he heard me.

CHAPTER 23
A STREET FIGHT

I climbed this ladder up a lot faster than the one I'd come down. At least I could see where I was going. Just before I reached the top, I looked back.

A pack of rats had come out of the darkness and were now feeding on the guy who I'd kicked in the head and the pieces of the corpses that were laying around. Well, I thought, maybe the guy these hobos were chewing on hadn't been dead when they got hungry.

It didn't make any difference anyway. The gang of bums had attacked me without any warning. If I hadn't killed a couple of them to get them off of me, I would of been dessert or maybe breakfast.

I moved the manhole cover back and came out into the street. There was no sign of Tor.

I expected that. It just had taken me too long to get through the tunnel.

I looked at my watch. It was 10:05. In an hour and fifty-five minutes Tor was going to kill Felicia. I didn't know why midnight was important for Tor to have his ceremony but I knew it was. He named midnight as though that was the only time that he could do what he was doing, to get the desired result.

I had to get Felicia away from him before then.

*   *   *

The rain was still pouring down and I was glad of it. The rain was washing off some of the stink and grime that had rubbed off on me during my fight with the hobos.

I sure as hell didn't have the time to run home and take a shower.

The street sign told me I was at Fifth Street and Vine. That was only two blocks from Roxie's.

It was back to plan number one. I trotted back to Roxie's through the pouring rain slipping and sliding through the puddles as I went. At Johnny's car I fished his keys out of my pocket and headed for the little hole in the wall nightclub called the Barbary Coast.

* * *

And so the circle turns. Three nights ago I came here to kill Morris West. He was not the one I should have come after. Tor Ambrose is the one who sends out the Morris West's of the world to do their dirty work. He just sits back and rakes in the profits. Tonight I come here to get information. If someone has to die for me to get that information, oh well, the circle turns now doesn't it?

I made one drive by to see what was going down on that block and to try to cut down on my surprises.

There was a prostitute on the corner huddled in a yellow raincoat. It was a slow night for that kind of thing. She must be pretty desperate.

There weren't many cars outside the Barbary Coast either so everything was real quiet.

My heart skipped a couple beats when I passed the alleyway. I didn't see anyone.

Then I did.

He was standing under the building's overhang back in the dark. It was my Morris West look-a-like in a shiny black raincoat.

I drove down the street, pulled into an alley. Then I backed out and turned around heading back the same way.

Time was short. I didn't want to look at any watch but knew time was passing. It was ten maybe fifteen minutes since I'd come out of the sewer.

I didn't have time to screw around tonight. Straight ahead was the only way I could afford to be with the clock ticking so fast. It was also the quickest way to get killed.

I pulled Johnny's car to the curb directly in front of the alley where the dealer was. I left Johnny's sawed off shotgun in the rider's side floorboard and after opening my door, I got out and came around the front of the car and walked directly to the alley. I walked straight into the darkness to where the dealer stood.

"What the fuck you want?" He demanded, hissing the words out like a pissed off Cobra.

I came right to him. There in the darkness, I jerked my Thirty-Eight out of my holster. I stuck the barrel under his chin.

The dealer froze. He put both of his hands up.

"This is how it is," I told him. "You're gonna tell me where Tor Ambrose lives. Then you're gonna climb your ass into my trunk. Cause if you're lying to me, I'm going to pump bullets into the trunk."

The dealer said, "Tor will kill me man."

I cocked the hammer back on my gun, "I'll save you the wait and do it right now if you don't tell me where Tor lives."

The dealer glanced over my shoulder at something in back of me.

"That ain't gonna work," I said. "I'm too close to you to be fucked. . ."

My head exploded from behind. A loud crack and I was thrown foreword. The dealer grabbed the gun out of my hand and hit me a glancing left uppercut as I went to the ground.

"Motherfucker always pulling guns on niggers," A familiar voice spoke from somewhere in the sky above me. "You ain't so tough now are ya motherfucker?" The voice said and I recognized it as Jamal. That kid whose nose I had broken a couple days ago.

"Thank you my brother," I heard the dealer say. "I will pay you back for the help."

Jamal tried to kick me in the stomach. I was almost unconscious but somehow got my leg up and blocked it.

"Fucker's got a hard head too," Jamal said, "Broke my board, clean in half."

"Get him up," The dealer spoke. Jamal got behind me and locked my arms into his and dragged me to a semi-standing position.

They dragged me out of the alley under the street light.

"I want to see your blood," the dealer said and he had the same fucked up Jamaican accent as all the rest of these assholes.

Jamal held me tight with my arms pinned behind me.

I was recovering real slowly this time. It might have been because I was so damn tired to begin with.

The dealer hit me with a jab square in the teeth and tried a left hook. I instinctively rolled with it and turned my head. He missed me completely.

"Hold him!" The dealer yelled.

"I am," Jamal said.

I laughed and that really pissed them off.

The dealer stuck my pistol in his pocket and pulled a long gleaming blade out.

He held the blade up for me to see. It was black and shined like glass.

"We kill with these," he told me with a gleam in his eyes. "Because they suck the soul up and give its power to us." He laughed loudly and said, "Get ready to die."

"Stop it!" A woman's voice screamed.

The dealer froze, and then looked over his shoulder at Lisa Rios. That had been her, standing on the corner. I recognized her now because the hood of her raincoat was pulled back. A big black purse swung on a long strap from her hand.

"Leave Mr. Dark alone," she yelled at them. She drew her purse back as though to strike at them.

"Go home, little girl," the dealer said and laughed.

"Yeah, bitch," Jamal said. "What you gonna do, hit us with your purse?"

The dealer turned back to me with a sneer on his lips.

Lisa whipped the purse around in a wide arc. It traveled in a circle around her head. It swung back, then forward. On its forward swing, she stepped forward and the purse smashed into the dealer's head with a loud thunk.

His head was rocked sideways and the dealer staggered.

"Damn," Jamal gasped and his grip loosened slightly.

I stomped down on his foot hard and felt his toe bones pop under my heel. I smashed the back of my head against Jamal's already broken nose and he screamed and let go of me.

The dealer staggered blindly and rammed his head against the side of Johnny's car. Lisa followed him and smashed him with another shot from her wicked purse.

The dealer went down like he'd been shot. Both his legs were stiff straight out and twitching.

I turned to Jamal and put my hands up.

He yelled, "Oh no, not the nose again!"

So I kicked him in the balls. He went down on his hands and knees.

I grabbed him by the back of his collar and the belt in the back of his pants and ran with him into the dark alley. I threw him as hard as I could and heard him bounce off of a dumpster in the darkness back there.

I walked back to where Lisa was looking down at the dealer. His head looked lopsided, like it had caved in on one side. Blood had run in lines from his nose down the sides of his face. His legs didn't twitch anymore. I checked the pulse on the dealer's neck. He was dead.

I turned to Lisa, "What the hell you got in that purse?"

"Just a brick," she said.

CHAPTER 24
A LOST CHILD

We were still the only ones out on the street. Around here, hearing screaming and yelling was nothing unusual. Nobody came out to investigate and unless there were gunshots nobody would even be curious.

I grabbed the dealer by his feet and dragged him back into the dark of the alley.

Lisa followed me.

"Damn. Damn. Damn," I muttered half under my breath. I took my Thirty-Eight out of the dealer's pocket and put it in my holster.

Lisa said in a small child's voice, "I'm sorry." After a pause she said, "Was he a friend of yours?"

"No, hell no!" I told her. "I needed to find out where his supplier lives. You see he's got this little girl he's going to kill at midnight. If I can't find him in time, she's dead."

Even in the darkness I could see Lisa's smile. "You're still out there saving little girls," she said. The memory flashed to me of how Lisa had clung to me the day I'd taken her away from those guys just outside Kansas City.

"If you're talking about Tor Ambrose," Lisa said. "I know where he lives."

*   *   *

In the darkness I heard Jamal moan from where he lay.

I spoke to him slowly and clearly so he would understand each word I said. "Jamal, If you ever fuck with me again I'm going to send you to meet Jesus. The next time we cross swords is the last."

Then I asked Lisa, "What's Tor's address?"

She said, "One night they came and picked me up to work a party for them. So I don't know the address but I can take you there."

We walked out into the light and I looked at my watch. It was about ten till eleven. I picked up the dealer's black bladed knife from where it lay and slipped it into my belt. "Let's go," I told her.

Lisa directed me where to drive and within a few minutes we were about five miles out of town where the houses were spaced farther apart.

Lisa turned to me in the car as I drove through the residential neighborhood toward Tor's house.

"Mr. Dark," she said. "How come you never took me up on my offer? You know I would do you for free."

We sat in silence for a few moments.

Then I told her, "Because I like you."

I could almost feel her smile.

She said, "I thought it was cause I was ugly or somethin."

"You're not ugly," I told her, "You're pretty."

I glanced at Lisa and saw that she was underweight. The crack that she was doing was taking its toll. She looked as tired as I felt.

We came to a neighborhood where there was a large patch of woods behind the houses. Each house was a good fifty to one hundred yards apart and all of them were large.

Lisa indicated a large black brick two story home with a patio over its double garage.

"That's it," she whispered. "Tor Ambrose lives there."

On the surface nothing looked unusual about the large house. The upper floor looked dark and lifeless. It had large plate glass windows and there was a sliding glass door from the balcony to the inner house.

But looking closely, I saw that the light coming through the curtained windows on the lower floor had a deep redness to it. There was a flickering to the illuminations within. I had no idea what kind of bulbs could create that kind of eerie effect.

The other thing that was not normal was the guy sitting on the porch in a lawn chair. He had a shotgun laying across his lap.

Around the house was a waist high chain link fence. Nothing unusual about that. To build a fence any higher would have been to attract attention. The last thing someone in an illegal business wants to do is attract attention.

I drove to the end of the block and turned to the side that Tor's house was on. At the end of that block was where the woods were. The woods border was the back property line of the houses. I parked there.

I started to get out of the car and Lisa started to get out too.

"Stay here," I told her.

"I'm coming with you," Lisa said.

"No," I told her. "I don't want you to get hurt."

"What," she said, "Are you serious? You're gonna tell me you care now!"

I looked at Lisa and saw the lost child she had never stopped being.

"You're not any different from anybody else," she said. "You don't give a fuck." A tear ran down her face. "You should have left me to die. At least it would be over now. I sell my ass on the street cause I have nowhere to go. No one to go to. Got no home, got no man, got no family. I wish I was just fuckin dead." The tears poured from her like a waterfall now and she covered her face with her hands.

I pulled Lisa to me and held her while her body was rocked with sobs. After a few moments she was able to calm down and catch her breath.

I don't know why I said it but I told Lisa, "You're gonna come stay with me."

I kissed her on the forehead and she drew back from me.

"You don't have to do that," she said wiping the tears from her eyes.

"I know I don't, "I told her. "We'll talk about this later. You know I've got to do this tonight."

I started to get out of the car, then as an afterthought, went back to her.

I told Lisa, "What I do need you to do is to call the police and get them out here. Tell them to tell Joe Briggs that I found Felicia and I'll need their help."

"I'll do that," Lisa said.

I reached over and smoothed Lisa's hair.

"Everything's gonna be all right," I told her.
She smiled. "I think it will be."
I went out into the rain.

CHAPTER 25
TOR'S HOME

Lightning and thunder crackled through the sky and shook the ground as I walked through the woods in back of the houses. I was wondering just what I had gotten myself into by telling Lisa I was taking her in.

The rain came down. The trees stopped most of it from getting down to me. I was thinking that I didn't really know Lisa Rios. I knew that she lived on the streets and did drugs but I assumed it was by choice. Maybe the way she lived was not her choice but just some way to make it from day to day.

This was not a romantic thing. Lisa had always been a kid to me and I would always see her like that. Well, I'd just help her out and see what would happen.

An Oriental voice in my mind spoke to me. The voice sounded like Me Ly and it said, "When you save someone's life you are responsible for them, because you changed their destiny." I wondered where I'd heard that before, probably *Charley Chan Theater*. Well, anyway I was going to help her and then just wait.

I could use the company anyway. Maybe I'd keep her from doing drugs and she'd keep me from drinking myself to death. Well maybe. There was no time to wonder about this shit now.

I came to the rear of Tor Ambrose's house. There was no sentry at the back door. But I guessed that was because there was no back porch. Who wants to stand outside and get soaked all night? Someone probably watches through a window.

I decided to walk to the far corner and climb the fence there. Then I would go up on the balcony above the garage.

When I got to the place where I was going to climb the fence, I realized I was going to have to throw the shotgun over to climb the fence fast. My hands were empty.

Right then I realized that I had left the shotgun in the floorboard of the car.

"What an idiot you are," I told myself.

There wasn't any time now to go back for it.

I felt for my Thirty-Eight in my holster.

It was there. Thank God I didn't forget that. I guess I'd forget my ass if it wasn't attached to me. My watch said eleven fifteen.

"Well now," I thought. "It comes down to this." I climbed the fence and dropped to the other side flattening myself in the grass.

Time to play.

* * *

There are reasons for all the things that I do. You may not understand them. I might not understand them, but there are reasons.

I sure didn't understand how I ended up on my belly crawling through some guy's backyard.

Blind luck, chance, fate, I didn't know. Maybe one, maybe all of them. Maybe none of them. Maybe the chess master in the sky just moves us around until he gets bored. Then he cleans the board off.

All I knew was I was going in that house, killing some people, and then taking Felicia home.

I tried to remember to crawl like I did in the Special Forces in Nam. To tell you the truth, I think all crawling is the same. You just keep your ass down.

I made my way to the blind side of the house where the garage was. An empty garbage can was next to the garage. It served as my stepladder to the balcony. I grabbed the balcony's railing with my hands and hoisted myself up. The rain was falling a little slower now but lightning shot down around the area like a fireworks display.

A hand grabbed me by the hair and I was jerked over the rail and flung to the balcony's carpeted floor with a thud. The wind was knocked out of me. All I could see in the rain and lightning was a large shape standing over me.

From my side on the floor I spun around and scissor kicked the guy, catching him behind the knees with my right foot and in front of his ankles with my left.

He fell forward but caught himself. I rolled away and came to my feet. The guy's pistol was on the floor and I kicked it. The gun flew off the balcony.

I started to draw my gun and realized if I fired everyone in the house would be up here and my ass would be dead real quick.

He got to his feet and I saw that my first impression had been correct. The guy was around six two and weighed around two hundred and twenty. He looked like he was in shape too. His rain soaked shirt told me this guy had quite a bit of muscle.

He came at me in silence and that was strange but that was what I wanted. He snapped out two jabs in my face and I barely slipped under an overhand right that had good-night written on it. I spun to the side and circled to my left.

This guy was fast.

The sequence of punches the guy had thrown showed me this guy had some good training behind him.

He missed with a left hook and I hit him with a straight right square to his nose. I tried a left hook that he backed away from.

The tall black guy had a grin on his face now. Well, that was great. He was enjoying himself. But I didn't have time for ten rounds of dancing and sparring. He wanted to box. So I played his game.

He came in with two left jabs again and this time I beat him to the punch with my own right hand. He grabbed me to clinch. This is where the rules stop, I thought. I brought my knee up into his groin. He didn't even grunt, so I did it again. His knees buckled.

Now I grabbed the dealer's knife from my belt and brought it around and buried it to the handle in his back.

He went down to his knees and his breath whooshed out of him. That was the only noise he ever made. So I ripped the knife out and buried it in his chest this time. He fell to his back. His eyes rolled up in his head, his mouth wide open like a silent scream.

Then I saw it as I looked in his mouth. He didn't have a tongue. It looked like his tongue had been cut out.

Why the hell had that been done, I asked myself. But there was no one to answer me and I would never know.

After wiping off the knife on his shirt, I slid it back into my belt.

I went in through a sliding glass door from the patio into the house.

*   *   *

The house was hot.

The air was thick.

When I say the house was hot, I mean it. Stepping into that upstairs room temperature wise was like stepping into a Mexican desert in August at noon. It must have been over a hundred degrees in there and it was a dry heat. If I hadn't have been as tired as hell already, which I was, the heat here would have made me that way.

The air was thick because it was smoky. A heavy haze hung in the air that burned my nostrils and my throat. Even though it had been a long time since I'd smelled it, I recognized the smell of that smoke right away. The smell was marijuana. These guys must have been burning it by the buckets downstairs to make it this smoky up here.

Stepping into this room was like stepping into a cave. It was extremely dark and it took me a moment or two to realize why. The walls were painted black and the only light was that weird flickering redness coming from below.

Past the doorway where the red light filtered through, I saw what looked like a staircase that led down. I drew my gun and moved toward it.

Through the floor beneath my feet, I felt as much as heard, a rhythmic drum beating. I wasn't going to be surprised if I saw some idiot with a bone through his nose banging on a bongo when I went down the stairs.

Tor was evidently trying to create the illusion of a voodoo ceremony taking place on a South Seas Island. He was doing a good job.

I went to the staircase where I was still in shadow and squatted and looked down on the scene below.

CHAPTER 26
BLOOD AND FIRE

The red light I saw right away was created simply enough by a red light bulb in the center of the ceiling.

There was a pentacle drawn on the floor. At each of its five points was a stand with a burning oil lamp. There was a large bowl that looked like a goldfish bowl on each stand also. Each of those had something in it that was dark red. I'm not a doctor but they looked like human hearts to me. They floated in a clear liquid.

At the foot of the pentacle was the guy who I'd heard beating the drum. That was what he was doing now. He was sitting cross-legged with another black man. Both were large and had on black T-shirts with blue jeans. Both were chanting something that sounded like:

"Astaroth, Astaroth, Sarganatos, Nebiros, Astaroth, Astaroth, Sarganatos, Nebiros . . ."

The pentacle was enclosed in a circle.

Tor Ambrose was bare chested with only a leopard skin loincloth on. He was at the head of the pentacle. He waved a black bladed knife in the air.

Felicia Richardson was naked and bound to stakes driven in the floor at four of the five points of the pentacle. I could see her weeping and mouthing the words, "No, No, No . . ."

I heard myself say, "This ain't gonna fuckin happen."

Tor raised his hands in the air and held the knife high overhead.

"Gods of darkness," he yelled and his voice boomed through the whole house. "I have opened the gate."

There was an answering loud crash of thunder and the house shook. The red light blinked off and on.

"I call on you," Tor shouted imploring the elements. "I call on you to come and take this gift. I give to you my own daughter's soul."

The lightning crashed four times in quick succession.

Felicia screamed.

"And as it was written," Tor continued. "You must, because of this offering, share your powers on earth with me. You must make me immortal."

Behind me I heard the floor creak.

I stood and spun around just in time to see someone rushing at me with a baseball bat. He swung the bat and I stepped backward, into space.

I had forgotten the staircase was now behind me. For only a moment I hung there then I let myself fall backwards. At the same time while falling I leveled my Thirty-Eight on the guy's face and pulled the trigger.

His head exploded like a ripe watermelon dropped from a building and I tumbled backward down the stairs. As well as I could, I rolled down the stairs all the way to the bottom. When I came to a stop at the foot of the stairs a shot blasted at me. A chunk of wood from a stair flew out beside my head.

It was the guy beside the drummer and I put a bullet in his throat. He went down choking and spitting blood.

The drummer dove for a rifle propped against the wall and I hit him between the shoulder blades. Then I shot him in the back of the head and his brains fairly exploded from the top of his skull.

The guy shot in the throat tried to get to his feet.

I took aim and pulled the trigger. The bullet roared through his forehead and his brains and blood smeared the wall behind him

I took aim at Tor, "You're dead motherfucker," I told him and pulled the trigger.

Just a hollow click. I was out of bullets.

Tor laughed. "You can't kill me," he said. "I'll never die."

The front door burst open and the guard rushed in. He leveled his shotgun at me.

"Hold it!" A voice yelled from behind him. The sound of another gun cocking was what I heard and Lisa Rios peaked at me from around the big man. She held the shotgun against the guard's back.

She said, "I thought you'd need me."

The guard jerked suddenly to swing the gun he had on her and Lisa let him have it with both barrels.

Chunks of the guard flew past me and he went down in two piles of red meat.

Tor reared back and threw the knife he had. It flew straight at Lisa.

I leaped to try and knock it away.

And missed.

Lisa screamed as the knife sunk into her chest.

I looked at her and she coughed blood.

"It hurts," she said weakly.

The sound of sirens came in through the open door.

"They're coming for you Tor," I told him. "They'll put you in a fucking cage where you belong."

He laughed. "Not after I do this," he said and drew another knife from the belt around his loincloth. He looked at Felicia.

"Time now," Tor said.

I grabbed one of the oil lamps from its stand and hurled it at Tor. It struck him full in the face and his head exploded in flames.

Tor screamed and stepped backward away from Felicia. I grabbed another lamp and smashed him with that one too. He screamed again and ran toward the back of the house flaming from head to toe.

I quickly untied Felicia and threw my jacket on her.

"Get out front," I told her.

I didn't have to repeat it. She moved fast outside.

Lisa was shaking as I picked her up and cradled her in my arms.

"It hurts," she kept saying to me.

I carried her out the front door, out the gate, and sat down with her on the grass. She was laying in my arms.

The police cars were arrived and I yelled at the first cop that came to us to get an ambulance.

The rain had stopped.

Lisa reached up and touched my face.

"I helped didn't I?" she said.

"I couldn't have done it without you," I told her. And it was no lie.

She was shaking in my arms.

"Do you think God will forgive me?" Lisa said.

"You earned it," I told her. "He will."

"Please hold me, I don't want to die alone."

I held her tightly in my arms and whispered, "You're not gonna die."

Lisa squeezed me back with her arms. Then her arms fell away and I felt the warmth leave from her face as I held her.

I started crying then and sometime later the ambulance crew made me let her go and they took her away.

Joe Briggs put his hand on my shoulder and I stood up.

"That was hard," he said.

We both looked at the sky. Tor's house was burning down around him. There was a rumbling from the clouds and a lightning bolt crashed down through the roof. The house exploded. The gods were not pleased with Tor.

CHAPTER 27
LOOSE ENDS

At the police department, Joe Briggs ushered me and Felicia to an office in the back of the station house. I gave Joe a quick rundown of what had happened that night.

Joe waited until Julia arrived before he got a statement from Felicia.

It took quite a while before Julia and Felicia could stop crying. When they did, Felicia, speaking to her mom, said that Tor told her he was her father. He got her to come out on the porch by showing her an old photo of him and Julia together. Then he forced her in a car.

Julia had never heard the name Tor Ambrose before, but she said she could not be sure that he wasn't Leroy Jones, her old boyfriend.

Joe took notes off of what we said, and then told us he had to make some arrangements. Then he left us alone in the room.

Julia and Felicia hugged each other and spoke in whispers.

Joe Briggs came back in about thirty minutes.

He looked directly at me and said he had made arrangements so I could walk away from the night clean.

"Our mutual acquaintance, Nash Graham, is going to take care of this," Joe told me.

Nash Graham is the DEA chief who hires me on occasions to remove problems for him.

"Nash is going to send out a team to take credit for a very bloody drug bust. The head of that team is Nash's son-in-law and the bust should get him the promotion he's been wanting," Joe said, then he smiled. "While you'd come out of this looking like a murderous maniac, they'll come out of it looking like brave hero cops. Makes sense, don't it?"

"It's good enough for me," I told him.

Joe turned to Julia then. "As far as the rest of the world knows," Joe told her. "Felicia came home on her own. If you say anything else, John might go to prison."

"She was with a cousin," Julia said, "And if someone asks too many questions, I'll just tell them to mind their own business and go away. Is that all right with you baby?" she asked Felicia.

Felicia nodded her head. She wasn't speaking too much and probably wouldn't for a while.

*   *   *

Joe Briggs took me into another room so we could have privacy for a few minutes.

"About what you say you saw in those five bowls in Tor's house, are you sure they were human hearts?" He asked me.

"That's what they looked like to me," I told him. "But hell they could have been dog hearts for all I know. They could have been store bought livers. I wasn't in no position to make an up close examination."

"Well," Joe said. "Keep it under your hat but I think you solved my five murder cases. What we never released to the press was that each of the five victims had his heart cut out. We'll know when we're done sifting through the ashes if Tor Ambrose was responsible for those murders too."

"In any case," I told Joe. "The world is better off without him."

"You got that right," he answered.

CHAPTER 28
A PROMISE OF REST

I walked Julia and Felicia up to their front door and stood there as Julia unlocked and opened the door. It was about four in the morning.

"You take it slow for a while," I told Felicia and reached out to pat her head.

She cringed away from me.

"That's all right," I told her and her mother.

"You go ahead inside," Julia told Felicia and she did.

She turned to me and looked in my eyes.

"I'm sorry about what happened to your friend," she said and I could see she meant it.

"Yeah, so am I," I told Julia. "She was just a kid," I said and then my voice broke and I couldn't help it. Tears ran down my face.

"I should have helped her a long time ago, but I didn't. I could of took her off the streets, but I didn't do anything."

The wind rustled the bush on my left and as tears ran down my face, Julia took me in her arms and gently held me.

When I regained control of myself Julia told me, "John, you look tired. Why don't you come in and get a shower and sleep on the couch. You might need someone to talk to when you wake up."

She was right. I couldn't remember ever feeling this tired. Every part of me ached. I had bruises on top of my bruises.

"I don't know," I said. Then immediately I said. "Of course I will."

Julia reached out and lightly ran her fingers over my cheek. She looked in my eyes. The wind rustled through the bush again.

She softly said, "When you let yourself be, you can be a really nice man."

"Don't ruin my reputation for me, O.K.," I told her.

Julia moved up against me and kissed me softly on my bruised tender lips.

A sharp, hot, searing pain erupted behind my left shoulder blade and I was thrown to the side.

A voice boomed in my ears, "She's mine."

My legs crumbled from beneath me and I found myself looking up at a very burned up, but very much alive Tor Ambrose. He held one of those black bladed knives in his hand. The blade was dripping with my blood.

Julia screamed, "Leroy, no!"

I tried to get to my feet and had no strength. Darkness washed over me. I tried to fight back the blackness that invaded my brain and I lost the fight.

Julia screamed again. Then I heard an explosion. I sank into darkness and silence.

*   *   *

Through a world of black I floated. Darkness was everywhere. I floated and drifted, going nowhere, not caring where I was or what was happening to me.

I wondered if maybe I would meet Kira here or maybe Lisa. But no one intruded upon my solitary dark world. Here I was alone.

CHAPTER 29
AWAKENING

Voices came to me. First as distant whispers, then as people speaking. Familiar voices speaking.

I opened my eyes.

Julia was sitting in a chair beside the bed. So was Felicia and that kid who has the hots for her, Terry.

"He's awake!" Terry said and came to stand beside me. "How ya feelin man?" he asked and clapped me on the left shoulder.

Pain vibrated through my entire left side.

"Ow!" I said. "Damn, why don't you just go ahead and hit me with a chair?"

"Sorry," Terry said.

Julia and Felicia came and stood around the bed beside me.

"Use your head boy," Julia told Terry.

"I think I'll survive," I told Terry. "Where am I?"

"St. Elizabeth's," Julia said. "You've been out for two days but it was due more to exhaustion than blood loss."

"Oh." I said.

Julia nudged Felicia and she came forward and stood beside me.

"Mr. Dark," she said. "I just want to thank you. You saved my life."

"No problem," I told her and stuck my hand up and she squeezed it, "Just a normal Tuesday night."

Then I told her, "They tell me you play a good game of chess."

Her smile was worth a million dollars.

"I'm OK," she said.

"You'll have to be better than O.K. to beat me kid," I told her, doing a rotten Humphrey Bogart imitation. "I'm the champ."

"You are?" Felicia said, "Until you play me." All three of them laughed and I knew that Felicia was going to come out of this all right.

A voice came from the other bed in the room.

"She is gonna beat ya. She's gonna beat you bad and I taught her every-thing she knows."

The voice was Johnny's.

"Oh no," I told the room. "I gotta share a room with him. I know I died and went to hell now."

"That's right," Johnny answered. "And I'm the boogie man. You ain't never gonna get away from me."

"Kids, I want to talk to John alone," Julia told the two teenagers and they walked to the door holding hands.

"Hey, Terry," I called out to him and he stopped and looked back at me.

"You better be good to her," I told him.

"It's the only way to be," he said as they went out the door.

"What happened at your front door?" I asked Julia and her face went se-rious.

"It was Leroy," Julia said. "When he stabbed you, I had to kill him."

"You certain he's dead?" I asked.

"Oh, yeah," Julia said. "I've carried a pistol for years. I put one right be-tween his eyes."

She was silent for a few moments.

"I'm sorry you had to do that," I told her.

"I'm not," she said. "He was gonna kill my little baby."

The door opened and a nurse came in.

She went to Johnny's bed.

"I am here to examine you," she said and I recognized the voice. It was Sushi.

She turned and winked at me then pulled the curtain around Johnny's bed.

"Terry's a good kid," I said to Julia.

"I know," she said. "He came to me respectfully like a man should. So I'm going to let him see Felicia."

"He gets stars in his eyes when he talks about her," I told Julia.

"Yeah," she said, "I really like that too. It's hard for me to accept, but my little girl is looking more like a woman every day."

We were silent for a moment or two.

From the next bed over, we heard Sushi's nurse uniform hit the floor.

"Oooh," we heard her say, "What is this thing I am finding down here?" She giggled.

"I don't know," Johnny said. "But it's growing."

Julia stifled a laugh. Then she looked at me seriously.

"I just want you to know," she said. "How much I appreciate what you did. Felicia is my life and you gave her back to me."

"I don't know how I'll ever pay you back," she leaned over and kissed me lightly on the forehead.

Someone moaned from the next bed and Sushi breathed, "I think I'm getting to the root of the problem."

Johnny said, "You definitely got the root."

We both laughed.

"That give you any ideas?" I asked Julia.

"No," she said. "I could never do that."

But she did have a smile on her face.

"I have to take the kids home," Julia told me. Then she leaned over and kissed me softly on the lips.

Julia walked to the door. Just before she left she turned and looked at me.

"Keep trying," she said.

Johnny moaned and said, "But I am trying."

"You shut up in there," Julia told him.

"Yeah," Sushi said. "You shut up and pay attention to me."

"Dominant women," Johnny said, "Oooh I love em."Then I had to lay there and try to sleep. There wasn't too much sleep to be had in that room that night.

CHAPTER 30
JULIA'S HOUSE

Three Weeks Later

Teddy Pendergrass is on the stereo.

Felicia is sitting across from me at the dining room table. A chess set is between us.

We are both drinking lemonade.

I reach out to touch my Bishop.

Felicia draws in her breath, hissing it between her teeth.

"Are you sure you want to do that?" She asks me.

I freeze then look into her eyes with mock seriousness, "Of course I want to do this," I tell her. "I'm beginning my final attack. I am going to begin a sequence now that spells total doom for your army."

I move my Bishop and grin at Felicia.

"Read it and weep," I say.

"You can take your move back if you want to," Felicia says.

"No way," I tell her. "You ain't gonna fool me. I can see you shiverin in your boots."

"OK," Felicia says. She moves her Knight and then says, "Checkmate in four moves."

"What?" I ask, I look closely at the board.

Felicia calmly explains the combination she has set up. I see there was no escape.

"Well, you cheated," I tell Felicia.

"No, I didn't," She says.

"Yeah," I said. "You're only supposed to use half your brain when you play me or it just ain't fair.

Felicia giggled.

"And now you laugh at me, too," I tell her. "That's great!"

Julia walked in the room and sat down at the table.

Felicia grins.

"You should take up child abuse," I tell Julia.

*　*　*

Later That Night

It's clear and cold. A light powdery snow is falling.

The black wrought iron gate screeched loud as I pushed it open. The air is chilly but there is no wind.

Funny, I think as I walk to Kira's grave, how the stars are out bright to-night and it's snowing.

The stars looked like jewels in the sky. Flickering points of light.

I walk across the graveyard and see the desolation. I see the remains of people that the world has forgotten. I carry two roses.

I would never forget.

I kneel down at Kira's grave and read the inscription: Kira Brooks, Rest in Peace.

I lay one of the roses on Kira's grave.

"Hello, Babe," I tell her. "Hope you don't mind me leaving a rose on Lisa's grave, but she was a good kid."

I look at the words on Kira's headstone again.

"I miss you so much," I tell her. "You know I never listened to you when you were alive. And I never really believed in God or angels or ghosts or anything like that. But I promise I'd listen now if you say anything at all. I'm ready now to listen. Really I am."

BOOK TWO

BOOK TWO

PART I

DEAD MEN
AND
GHOSTS

Caligula publicly expressed his
horror at what he called,
"This most bloody Murder."
-   From Gladiators by Michael Grant

Do not attempt to see order
In this world.
All is Chaos.
All is Chaos.
From the largest star
Down to the tiniest ant
All things are
In the end
Devourers.
-   The Mad Arab

CHAPTER 31
FEBRUARY 4, FRIDAY

The world is just full of surprises. Flowers bloom, birds sing and wonderful things just seem to spring up in front of you without any warning. At least that's what they tell me.

This morning as the phone rang and the sun shined, birds must have been singing somewhere. If I'd seen those little bastards they would have chirped their last note.

I had a roaring headache. The sun was like torture. The flowers could kiss my ass for all I cared. I felt like shooting the phone.

Maybe I'll just go and shoot whoever's calling me, I thought.

Last night I had a fight with Jack Daniels.

Jack won.

He always does.

I forced myself to get off the couch and stumbled over to the phone. On the way over I reached inside my boxer shorts and scratched my balls. My hangover was so bad even they hurt. I had to stop and think for a moment and try to remember if my sore balls were the result of some carnal adventure I'd had last night.

No, I didn't fuck anybody last night. It was a shame because I'd been going through a long dry spell and even if I couldn't remember last night, hell she might still be asleep in my bad. I'd give her a morning sausage breakfast before she knew what she was being fed.

Well, no sense in thinking about that. The way my head was pounding I wouldn't give a shit if Miss America was in my bed. I'd just fart in her face and tell her to hit the bricks.

I picked up the phone.

"This better be fucking good," I said to whoever was on the other end of the line.

"This is Graham Nash," the gravelly voice came back. "Sounds like you're having a good morning."

Graham Nash was the head of the D.E.A's Midwestern Department. He occasionally calls me and gives me work.

"You woke me up," I told him. "I was dreaming I was fucking your wife."

"You should thank me then," he said. "That must have been a really bad nightmare."

"OK, What's up?"

"Got some work for you, John," Graham said. "So, are you in the mood to make some money?"

He knew the answer to that question.

"I'm only in the mood to take a shit and throw up," I told him. "Meet me at Johnny's in about an hour."

"I'll be there," Graham said and hung up.

* * *

I wasn't joking about needing to take a shit and throw up. I made my way to my throne with my stomach making squishy growling noises the entire way. I sat down and spread my ass cheeks and let loose with a flood of flying shit that had the consistency of watered down chocolate pudding.

About a gallon and a half of this crud that smelled like hell on earth spurted from my asshole before I was done with that part of this morning's adventure in bodily evacuation.

I felt about five pounds lighter. But the adventure wasn't over yet. I tried to stand up and my stomach instantly spasms.

I instinctively hit the flush lever. I knew where my face was going in a few seconds.

Turning around and looking at the swirling shit made my head swim. The swirling motion of the liquid shit made me dizzy as hell. Then, I realized it wasn't going down.

The crap was coming back up to visit me.

It was all I could do to keep from spewing my guts up and there was no way in hell I was sticking my head down there.

Holding my mouth shut and doubled over from the waist I stumbled over to the window. I threw the window open and stuck my head out into the East St. Louis winter. The cold hit me in the face like a slap. I wretched out a long stream of greenish vomit. My stomach felt empty at last.

From below me came a yell and a curse.

"Hey, you motherfuckin' bastard," someone yelled.

I opened my eyes and saw below that I had just woke up some wino by throwing up all over his head.

"Get a bath," I yelled back at him. I pulled my head in and closed the window.

Jesus, I thought, what a fucking morning. Well, it could have been worse. I could have been that guy outside.

*　　*　　*

East St. Louis in the winter is not a pretty place. Come to think of it, East St. Louis in the springtime isn't so good either. Today the sun was bright. Too damn bright! The snow was dingy and dirty. Piles of trash were partially covered by the old snow.

I had a headache that was like an ax in my brain. Before I'd showered, I'd taken six aspirin. They didn't help. Even combing my hair hurt this morning.

At Johnny's place, I almost fell through the door. I walked over to where Graham was sitting at the bar. He was taking a drink of his beer and making a face.

Johnny was behind the bar. *I Dream of Jeannie* was on the TV.

He said, "Bet that girl's got a bush an anaconda snake could get lost in. And I know the snake that'd like the job of explorin' that jungle."

Graham held up his beer to me. "This stuff tastes like piss water," he said.

Without so much as turning his head Johnny said, "I pissed in that glass just for you. That's the part that'll give you the buzz."

"Is he always like this?" Graham asked and motioned at Johnny who was making faces at Jeannie like he was fucking her.

"Yeah," I said. "Except when he's in church, then he's worse."

"I say what you think," Johnny said and turned his prune like face toward us. "You all know you want to fuck Jeannie, but now you act like she ain't good enough for your dick." He looked back to the screen and blew a kiss.

"I have some work I need done," Graham said his voice hardening.

This must be something serious, I thought. Graham had hired me several times before to dispose of problems for him. He was the kind of guy who'd tell jokes while his friends bled to death. But his attitude this time was dead serious.

"You all have to discuss that shit somewhere else," Johnny told us. "Last time I got mixed up in John's business I spent a week in the hospital."

I told Johnny, "I thought you wanted to be a hero that night."

"Well, I did," he said. "Right up until I got cut."

"It wasn't all bad," I told him. "Remember Sushi did fuck the hell out of you."

"That's right," he said. "It was good too, but damn, she busted all my stitches open. Most of that moaning you heard was pain."

Graham was growing impatient. "Let's take a walk," he said and we moved toward the door.

Johnny was back to watching Jeannie's ass.

"John," he shouted from behind the bar. "Stop by Jose's and bring me back five tacos."

"Who says I'll be back," I shout back.

"You will," he answers.

CHAPTER 32
MONEY IS MONEY

We didn't talk much on the way over to Jose's.

Graham made a few comments about how attractive the neighborhood was. He'd point at a boarded up building or an overflowing dumpster and say, "Urban renewal is in full force here. And I do see that it makes a difference."

But for the most part he was silent as we walked through the grim cold streets of the crumbling city.

It was only about two blocks to Jose's but I felt about half frozen before we got there. The sun was shining like a laser beam into my head. It may have been bright but the sun wasn't warm.

We opened the door to Jose's and the smell of Jalapenos and fried meat rushed out to meet us. I realized right then that I was hungry.

Jose's has heavy wooden benches instead of chairs and big thick wooden picnic tables. We sat down. The floor was dusty and the lighting was dim. Bull horns were hung high up on one of the walls. Other things were hung on the walls that were supposed to look Texasy. It didn't matter to me if it looked like we were in Hong Kong. This stuff smelled good.

A fat, sweaty looking Mexican guy with a small notepad in his hand came over to our bench.

He wiped his nose with his hand then wiped his hand on the front of a shirt that had once been white. Now the shirt was kind of yellowish, especially near the armpits.

He dropped two menus on the table, glared at us and walked away.

"Friendly service," Graham said.

"Well, the cook don't have to be pretty for the food to be good," I told Graham.

Graham reached in his shirt pocket and took out a photograph. He slid it across the table to me. "Address is on the back," he said.

I picked up the photo and looked at it. It looked to be a D.E.A. Surveillance picture. The photo was of a young man standing on a street corner. He was slim, had a clean cut handsome face and short, well-trimmed blond hair. Even in the grainy photograph I got a sense that this was no hardened criminal. Not like the usual problems I'm used to removing.

Graham picked up the menu. I looked at the picture and the menu.

"Stay away from the tamales," I told Graham. "They put extra peppers in them. Eat those, you'll be shittin' fire."

"I'll get some tacos," Graham said. "The usual fee right?"

This was unusual. Graham never asked anybody anything. He was used to telling people what to do, not asking. This, as well as his tense attitude, and the guy in the picture not looking anything like a hard-core criminal, made me feel like something was wrong with this job. But, hey, money is money.

"Price just went up," I told Graham. "You're not acting normal. That tells me that something is different about this hit."

Graham's face colored red for a moment and he looked away toward the bullhorns on the wall.

He turned back to me, "How much?"

"Double," I said.

Graham flushed red again, "This one will be easier than your normal jobs."

"You even saying that worries me," I told him.

A waitress came to the bench. She was large, to put it mildly. They must have good food here, I thought. This girl is well fed.

"I'll take a Tecate," Graham said, "And three beef tacos."

She looked at me with almost disdain on her face.

"Give me a Corona," I said, "And I'll take five beef tacos."

She wrote the orders down slowly. She looked back to Graham. "The meat will be hot," she said and winked at him. Then she turned and walked through the door to the kitchen.

"I think she's in love," I told Graham.

"That is scary," he said. "I won't pay you double."

"Everything is negotiable," I said.

Our waitress came back with the beers. She smiled at Graham and gave me the evil eye.

She went away.

"Six thousand," Graham said.

"Nine thousand," I answered.

"Shit," Graham said. "Split the difference, seven thousand five hundred."

I took a big swig of my beer. It was cold and good.

"I'll do it," I told him. "With one condition. Half now, half later."

"Agreed," He said. "I'll send someone around tonight to slip an envelope under your door."

"Good!"

Graham took a long drink of his beer. He stuck out his hand and I shook it. "One other thing," he said while still gripping my hand. "Make him die slow."

"I'll consider it," I told Graham and pulled my hand back.

CHAPTER 33
DOMESTIC BLISS

After we ate, mostly in silence, I ordered five more tacos and went back to Johnny's.

Johnny looked in his bag of tacos and said, "Where's my Picante Sauce?"

"You didn't say you wanted any," I said. "Besides you smell bad enough already without me adding fuel to the fire."

"You know I like Picante. You could have brought me some," he said.

"Kiss my ass," I told him.

"Move your face," he came back.

"I'll kick your ass," I told Johnny.

"Yeah, you and who's army," he said.

"Mine," I said. "Get the set."

Johnny reached beneath the bar and brought out an old battered chess set. He set it up on a table and commenced war.

"Today I got your ass," he said under his breath as he made his first move.

At least my headache is gone, I thought as I made my first move.

Today Johnny was good. I tried my tricks and he fended off my attacks rather easily. We were on our third game and he'd won the first two when Johnny asked, "What's up between you and that girl, Julia, lately? Seems like you've been hanging around here a little too much."

"Ain't nothin up between us," I told him. "Julia told me if I was going to be around her and Felicia I needed to stop the drinkin. Hell, I ain't lettin no woman tell me what to do."

"Then you're an idiot," Johnny said.

"She said that, too."

Johnny moved his knight. I moved another pawn forward to free up some pieces to attack with. It may have not been a great idea to open up my king row as much as what I was, but today, I seemed to be short on ideas. We sat in silence for a while. I took a drink of my beer. Johnny took a drink of his.

"So what's up between you and Sushi these days?" I ask.

"None of your fuckin business," Johnny said.

"Well, that's good," I tell Johnny. "You ask me questions, I give you answers. I ask you a question, I get shit."

"Some things are personal."

"No shit," I told him.

Johnny was looking deeply into the chess board. "She told me I should improve my life," he said. "She says I should either make this place into a nightclub with entertainment or turn it into some kind of a sports bar with pool tables and a big screen TV so better people come in here."

"Maybe you should," I said.

"Shit," Johnny said. "For me to get better people in here I'd have to bus them in from out of town. You know nobody with any money and half a brain comes to East St. Louis."

"That's why we're here," I said.

"You got that right," he answered. "And the brilliant ideas about how I should improve my life came from a woman who shakes her bare ass in a tittie bar."

"Don't tell me you told her that," I said.

"Yeah, I guess I did," Johnny said. "It wasn't one of my smartest moments."

I made another move and told Johnny I was going to checkmate him in about five moves.

"You're full of shit," he said.

Maybe he was right.

* * *

I played chess with Johnny till about nine o'clock in the evening. He won most of the games. I left and got in my car and cruised the streets. I didn't have anywhere I wanted to go, so I just drove around.

I found myself gliding past Julia's house. The flickering light of a TV set was all that was on inside. It would be so much warmer in there, I thought.

I wondered why I had to drink so much. No answer came to me. I drove on toward my empty home.

*　　*　　*

An envelope with three thousand seven hundred and fifty dollars was just inside the door of my apartment.

I counted it carefully.

Twice.

I took the photograph out and looked at it again. This guy could have been any young dude in his first year of college. He looked like he had not lived a hard life. There was a softness about his face and about his posture. This guy was used to the good life and not used to working for it.

I wonder what he did to deserve what I was going to do to him. It was best just to do the job and not think about that.

The address on the back of the photo read, Robert Perry, 2020 Division Street, Pontoon Beach, Illinois. It wasn't that far away. Maybe fifteen minutes.

The time was about ten thirty. I didn't feel like sleeping. I sure didn't feel like drinking myself to sleep. For some reason the whiskey bottle just didn't seem too inviting tonight. So I decided to take a ride out there and take a look at the scene of a murder.

CHAPTER 34
A TOWN THAT SLEEPS IN SILENCE

Pontoon Beach is a small sleepy village east of St. Louis. Not too much goes on there. Anyone from Pontoon Beach who wants to do anything leaves town to do it. There really is nothing there but a couple of small town bars. I can't go near any of those bars.

I have to be invisible.

I cruise the streets. There are very few streetlights and lots of trees. The streets are dark so every time I come to a street sign, I have to slow down and almost stop to read the street names.

I wonder why they call this town Pontoon Beach. There's not a beach anywhere and the only water I see is a murky lake that only the suicidal would swim in.

I drive slowly through the streets of this half dead town. Sometimes dogs bark, but mostly there is just a heavy silence. Sometimes I see the blinking lights of TV sets in the houses. The silence is like the breathing of a giant in his sleep.

Division Street.

I turn onto it and drive down it slowly. It's one of the darkest streets in this town. Which means it's nearly pitch black. This is good for me.

Mail boxes are almost all the way out in the road. I look for the address on them.

After about six mailboxes set in front of houses that were way back in very large lots with long gravel driveways, I see 2020. No name is on the mailbox. I drive slowly past the house. No lights shine from the house. It's completely black back there. Good for me.

About ten houses down there's a house that is closer to the street than the others. It's more of a shack than a house. It looks like it's ready to cave in on itself. It's obviously deserted. I park in front.

I take a pair of old cloth gloves out of the glove compartment of my Olds Delta Eighty-Eight. After putting these on, I walk by the side of the road back to the driveway of 2020. It's so dark I can barely see my feet on the pavement. The driveway is white gravel. At least I can see the ground from here.

The house is a one level white brick home with a garage on its left side. I try the windows on the side of the house.

They're locked.

I try the windows at the back of the house with no luck. At the kitchen was a big glass sliding door. I try it. It is locked.

There is an outside entrance door to the garage. This door is unlocked. This room was as black as the darkest pit of hell. I felt my way along the wall and scoot along trying not to run into a shelf and somehow find a door leading inside.

I felt a light switch on the wall. I switch it on to scan my surroundings. A door was right beside me. I switch off the lights and turn the door knob. The door opens.

I step onto the linoleum floor of the kitchen. No lights on inside. I'd seen this from outside. But compared to the blackness of the garage, I felt like I had stepped out into the morning sun.

I went to the sliding glass door and flipped the latch, opened the door, then shut it again.

There was a table with four chairs in the center of the kitchen. A glowing digital clock on the front of a microwave oven told me that it was eleven thirty five. Time to wait. I sat down in one of the chairs and looked out into the darkness.

The nightclubs in this area usually close around two o'clock. I would expect this guy I'm waiting for, Robert Perry, to stay out at least that late. Of course the clubs in Washington Park never close. Or maybe this guy could find a girl to spend the night with. In which case, he may not come home at all. Either way, there was nothing for me to do but wait.

This Pontoon Beach was a small town. I wondered what it would be like living out here. This place was quiet. It seemed like people kept to themselves. Could I live in a place this quiet, I wondered. I was used to hearing ambulance sirens at all hours of the night. I could hear gunshots at noon or two o'clock in the morning. Drunks slept in the alleyway beneath my window. Which wasn't such a good idea.

Out here, life was slow. People don't bump into each other. Where I live people bump and shove, sometimes with shoulders and elbows, sometimes with fists or bullets.

I sit here in Pontoon Beach in a dark kitchen and wait. Life is slow here. No cars drive by out in the road. People live to be old out here, but they are probably dead a long time before they make it to the grave.

*   *   *

The light in the kitchen comes on and Julia Richardson is standing across the room from me. Felicia her daughter stands beside her. Julia is looking tall and proud, her chocolate skin almost seems to glow. Felicia looks very much like her mother, only about five inches shorter. Neither of them is smiling.

"I see that you are chasing death again," Julia says so quietly it is almost a whisper.

"It's what I do," I answer and for no reason that I know of my heart starts pounding hard in my chest. It feels like I've run a long distance. I feel what is almost a sense of panic settle over me.

Felicia smiles, "Do you want to play some chess?" she asks and points to the table in front of me.

I now see that a chess set is on the table. The set is made of white and black marble. The pieces are large fine detailed sculptures of skeletons.

Felicia's smile now looks strangely hungry. "It makes no difference who wins," she says almost giggling. "The end is the same."

A hand touches my shoulder and I see that Kira Brooks, my girlfriend who now lies in a grave, is standing beside me.

She kisses me on the cheek. Her lips are large and warm. "They will join me soon," she says and the skin on her face turns to dust and falls away to reveal a grinning skull beneath.

I scream and jump to the side.

Julia and Felicia start laughing and their skin starts melting from their bodies.

They both start chanting together, "Our turn soon! Our turn soon!"

I scream again and run into a wall.

My eyes open and I'm staring at the linoleum floor that I have fallen on-to. The sun is streaming in through the sliding glass door.

I come awake with a jarring suddenness. I almost spring to my feet. The house around me is quiet. The only sound is the chirping of birds outside.

It's not easy but I make myself calm down. My breathing slows down and my heart stops racing. I just can't believe it. I had actually fallen asleep in a guy's house that I came out to kill. If that ain't about the stupidest thing imaginable to do, then I don't know what is.

So Robert Perry had never come home. A good thing for me too. They might have found me snoring like a baby rhino and with my luck he'd have brought the whole Pontoon Beach Police Department home with him for beers.

I looked around the kitchen and saw a blank note pad sitting on the coun-ter. There was indention's in the paper where the sheet above had been written on and torn off. Something made me want to know what had been on that note pad.

A long time ago, I'd seen on an episode of *Perry Mason* where he'd taken a pencil and rubbed lightly on a note pad just like this. That showed the words that had been written on the page that had been torn off. I started looking through drawers in the kitchen for a pencil. Then I saw stuck to the refrigerator with a magnet, a sheet of paper from the note pad.

The message on the paper read, FLT.162, Feb, 4, 10:00 P.M. Return, FLT 159, Feb 9, 10:00 P.M.

Below that was wrote Atlanta Hilton, the telephone number and confir-mation number.

Well, it appears as though my boy isn't coming home anytime soon.

CHAPTER 35
NAKED WOMEN AND IDIOTS

I took the note and went back to my apartment. Sleeping in that chair gave me a real bad backache. I climbed in bed to stretch out for a while and woke up about three hours later feeling a lot better.

It was about twelve thirty in the afternoon, so I dialed Graham Nash's number. I expected to get his answering machine since it was Saturday, but he answered on the second ring.

"Graham," he said.

"John Dark," I answered. "Subject left town."

"Go get him," Graham said.

"It'll cost an extra thousand to go after him."

"You're over paid already," Graham said.

"That's the cost," I said.

"Do it," Graham said without hesitating. "It will be included in your final payment."

Both of us hung up without another word.

I called Lambert Airport and reserved a seat on a flight to Atlanta, Georgia. The flight didn't leave till noon on Sunday, the next day.

Without even thinking about it, I called Julia's number. She answered on the third ring.

"Just wanted to know if you were doing all right," I told her.

"Thanks," she said, "I'm always doing all right."

"I've been thinking a lot about you."

"Yeah," Julia answered. "I think about you some too."

There was a heavy silence between our words.

"Stop by," she said. "We'll talk about things."

"I will," I told her.

*   *   *

About eight o'clock that night I found myself at Johnny's and we played chess for a while. I took revenge for the beating I took the night before. After I whipped him four games straight Johnny announced he wanted to head out.

There was one drunk in the place half asleep on the bar. We ran him out and Johnny locked up. I rode with Johnny in his car to a place named Dottie's Body Shop. It was a little strip club just outside the city limits of East St. Louis.

Johnny didn't want to go out to Roxie's tonight. Sushi was working. Ever since they had been sleeping together, Johnny couldn't stand seeing other guys look at Sushi when she took her clothes off on stage.

She wants Johnny to change his life and he wants her to change hers. It doesn't look like either one of them is going to budge one bit.

Dottie's Body Shop was actually just little more than a bar with a stage in the center of it where one woman was dancing. The lighting was dim except for a spotlight that was shining on the stage.

There were three waitresses wearing bikini bottoms and nothing else. All three looked young, almost like children. They tried to smile when they served the drinks but mostly they wore sad expressions on their faces.

The music was from a jukebox. The sound was tinny and the words were impossible to understand. The drinks were overpriced and watered down. A large black bouncer sat at the bar.

I ordered a coke.

"You must be sick tonight," Johnny said.

"I just don't feel like drinking tonight," I told him.

There were about twenty guys in the place and they were of the quiet drinking type. No one was at the stage where a slim waiflike girl danced with an energy that was almost sleep inducing.

"You brought us to an exciting place," I told Johnny. "They should call this the zombie strip club."

"Well, I got my reasons," Johnny said.

I know Johnny just wanted to avoid seeing Sushi. He should have chosen a different club.

We received our drinks and our waitress tried her best to impress us by wiggling and giggling and generally acting like a mentally defective juvenile delinquent. It was pretty pathetic.

She made me feel so sorry for her I gave her a two dollar tip. The way she wiggled from the excitement of getting that money made me think she just had an orgasm.

This place was really damn dreary.

The door swung open and a young guy who looked like a short weight lifter and an older guy who looked like a little old cab driver came in. The young guy went directly to the stage and made a grab for the dancer's leg. She jumped back from him.

He laughed real loud and yelled, "I want some pussy." The young guy had moved with an athletic grace that showed he wasn't drunk no matter how stupid he was acting.

The older man sat down beside the younger guy. He was shaking his head in disapproval but was ignored. The bouncer came from the bar and said something to the young guy who just laughed it off and waved it away.

"That guy is a fucking idiot," Johnny said.

"Yeah," I answered. "There are enough of them around."

The girl kept dancing but she kept here distance from the idiot. He kept laughing loudly and acting like an escapee from the monkey house.

I took a drink of my coke. Johnny took a drink of his beer.

I looked around the room then looked at Johnny. Johnny looked around the room then looked at me.

"Are you going to want to stay here long?" I asked Johnny.

He held his beer up to me. "I'll drink this," he said. "And we'll get the hell out of here."

"Next time you want to avoid Sushi," I told Johnny. "We'll just hang out at the mortuary. We could find more life in that place than we could here."

The girl on the stage danced two more songs and then left.

I got a bad feeling in my stomach when the bouncer got up on the stage.

"Christ, don't tell me he's gonna dance," Johnny said. "They can't be that desperate for some entertainment here."

The bouncer spoke loudly so everyone in the room could hear him.

He announced, "Now appearing by special arrangement the Jewell of the Orient, the Wild and Wonderful Star of the Far East, directly to you, Sushi."

I looked at Johnny and Johnny looked at me, "No shit," he said.

I could tell right then, this night was going downhill.

Sushi climbed up on the stage and started dancing to her signature song Kung Fu Fighting. She was a small athletic woman wearing a kickboxing outfit complete with hand wraps.

She started going through her Kung Fu Fighting routine. Sushi was kinda short and kinda skinny but the way she was snapping out punches and kicks she looked like she could really kick some ass.

Sushi was twirling around and snapping punches and kicks and dropping clothes along the way. Johnny was looking pissed off. Midway through the song Sushi and Johnny locked eyes just after she had dropped her bra.

Johnny's face expression changed from smoldering anger to extreme sadness. Sushi saw this. Her gaze dropped to the floor and she involuntarily tried to cover herself with her arms. She looked like she was going to cry as she froze beneath the spotlight.

Johnny stood up and took off his jacket and walked to the stage where Sushi stood like a shamed statue. He started to climb up on a chair and ascend to the stage when the young idiot grabbed his arm.

"I came here to see a show, motherfucker," he yelled at Johnny.

He was grabbed by the bouncer who pulled him aside and yelled, "I done told you about being stupid in here boy. You're leaving now!"

"Fuck you," he yelled back.

Johnny climbed to the stage and put his jacket around Sushi.

"Keep a low profile," I heard the old guy with the young idiot say.

"Well fuck you too!" He yelled at him.

I was going to make sure Johnny and Sushi wasn't messed with, so I walked toward the stage.

In the next second I recognized who the young guy was. He wrenched himself out of the bouncer's grip and stepped back one step.

The bouncer reached for him.

It was a bad mistake.

The young idiot was a boxer that I'd seen climb up through the rankings for the last couple years. He was Roy Wilson, a top ten contender for the middleweight title.

Roy Wilson did a move I'd seen him do at least a dozen times on TV. He dipped and slipped to the left side, then whipped a hard left hook to the bouncer's jaw. The bouncer staggered sideways, then went over a table and crashed to the floor.

Wilson moved in Johnny and Sushi's direction and I was directly in his way. He had a look on his face that was like bloodlust. He wasn't going to stop until a lot of people were hurt or he was stopped.

"It's my turn boy," I told Wilson and readied myself for him.

"I'll fuck you up," he said and came at me.

But I had a big advantage. I knew who he was, but he didn't know me.

He stepped in and did his little dip to the side and I was expecting it. When he whipped his left hook I'd already stepped inside it. His left fist went behind my head.

I shoved him backward with my shoulder. When he straightened up to keep his balance, I blasted him with a straight hard right cross. The punch drove him to his back. Blood spurted from his nose.

We didn't need a referee to count to tell us that this bout was over.

*　　*　　*

I drove Johnny's car back to his bar. Johnny left with Sushi in her car.

They mumbled thanks to me for what I had done to Roy Wilson.

"No thanks necessary." I told them. "He needed getting knocked on his ass and I enjoyed doing it."

The last glimpse I got of Johnny and Sushi that night was when I looked back at them and they were sitting in the front seat of Sushi's car. By the light of the dashboard I could see Johnny reach out and tenderly touch Sushi's face with his fingertips. He was saying something to her and it looked like a tear ran down his face.

CHAPTER 36
BOOKS

I checked in at Lambert Airport the next morning at ten thirty. The plane didn't leave until noon. Why was I here so early?

Sometime in my life, someone had told me you need to check in at least an hour early to take a flight. So it took me five minutes to get through the line and now I had an hour and a half to stand around and feel kind of stupid because I was here so early.

I went walking around the shops looking at things, souvenirs mostly. What do I need with a souvenir? I live here. I guess I could buy a plastic Gateway Arch and sit it in the window so all the winos could see I have civic pride.

I went in a little bookstore and started looking through the paperbacks they had there. The science fiction books were of worlds that never were and never would be. Maybe I did need some place to escape to, I thought as I looked at the covers of the books. There were pictures of muscular guys with swords and beautiful women in almost no clothes fighting ugly creatures.

I do enough fighting in my life I thought, so I don't want to fantasize about it. I went past those.

Then there were the romances. No, I don't think so.

The lady behind the counter was the studious type. She looked tall and slender with short chestnut brown hair. She had wire rimmed glasses that set off the color of her green eyes. She had on one of those loose type summer dresses with a flower print on it. It was February outside but in here, spring was in bloom.

She saw me looking around the store with no success. Now she stood up and held a book out to me. "You look like a mystery man," she said.

"That I am," I answered and couldn't help but look down her dress at her smallish round breasts as she leaned forward. Just the right size for my mouth, I thought and round just like oranges.

She blushed and laughed and I took the book from her hand. The name of the book was *Hard Road Ahead.* The cover showed a man standing outside a Fifty-Seven Chevy Convertible with a vixen of a brunette in the front seat showing off her legs.

He was holding a pistol in his hand and both of them were looking down a two lane road into the sunset.

I read the back cover writing out loud to the woman at the counter.

"He was a two fisted private detective with a dame he couldn't trust. His past was violent and his future is just a long ride down the hard road to nowhere."

The lady behind the counter smiled and her wire rimmed glasses made her look like she always had something on her mind.

"It sounds like my biography," I told her and I went to hand her the book back.

She put her hands up. "No charge," she said. "I brought it from home, but it's not my type of book."

"Well, Judi," I said seeing her name tag. "Thank you." Then I walked toward the door holding the book. I stopped near the entrance and looked back. Judi had her back to me. Her loose dress outlined the shape of the curve of her back and her ass. She looked good.

"Hey," I said to her and she looked at me over her shoulder. I held the book up, "*Here's looking at you kid,*" I said in my best Bogart.

Judi laughed. "If you want anything, just whistle. You know how to whistle, don't you? Just put your lips together and blow."

"That I will."

*   *   *

My flight left on time.

It was a cloudy, dreary, snowy day, but in no time we were above the clouds. I got a drink from the stewardess. One of those midget bottles of Jack Daniels.

I opened up my book, *Hard Road Ahead*, and read for a while. I ended up skimming through it. Max Thursday was the detective. He was hired to follow a man, to catch him cheating on his wife and to report everything to his wife, June. June started an affair with Max and Max found out that June's husband, Juan, was dealing drugs in a big way. The story was set in the border town of Nogales, Arizona. June set Max and Juan against each other. After Max killed Juan, she took off with Juan's money and Max went to jail.

Well, you just never know about women, I thought and put the book down. You just never know. The only thing that was certain was that Max was a dummy.

The plane landed and taxied into the terminal.

CHAPTER 37
YOU JUST NEVER KNOW

I had a taxi take me out to the Atlanta Hilton. The first thing I noticed about Atlanta was that it was hot.

During February in St. Louis the highs are usually a maximum of forty degrees. I got off the plane and it was sixty-five.

The highway was packed. It took about a half hour to make it to the hotel. I got out of the cab, paid the cabbie, and watched him drive away. I walked to the Ramada across the street carrying the one suitcase I brought with me.

I checked in at the Ramada and made sure they gave me a room on the first floor. Once, I'd done a job in Detroit and the body was found quicker than I'd anticipated. The police did a door to door search of that hotel and the one next door.

I was in a second floor room of that hotel next door. There was no way I could explain the unregistered gun I had with me. That night I jumped from the second floor window and nearly broke my ankle, but the police hadn't covered the alley.

I didn't want to be hopping out of any more windows.

I opened up my suitcase and set it open on the dresser. Inside the suitcase I arranged my stuff so I could use them from right inside the suitcase. If I had to leave fast I didn't want to be having to pack anything.

That done, I turned on the TV. There wasn't much on. Just a few old sitcoms and a couple of southern preachers throwing out fire and brimstone. On one channel they were showing that old movie, *Gone With The Wind*. That's really what I needed to see right now. Some southern asshole trying to fuck some chic who doesn't want to have shit to do with him and then when she finally does want his dick, he doesn't want her pussy anymore. Hell, I'd have fucked her just so I could tell her to hit the bricks just to piss her off worse. But hey, that's just me, and I hadn't been fucked in so long that even the crack of dawn gives me a hard on. And about that movie, frankly my dear I just don't give a damn.

I turned off the set.

It was five o'clock in the afternoon, no, make that six o'clock. Now I'm in Eastern Time so I reset my watch an hour later.

After waiting in the airport, then waiting while flying to get here, I didn't want to just wait all night in the hotel room before I could get to checking the situation.

So I decided to go down to the lounge and have a drink.

I walked around the first floor looking for the lounge and didn't find one. All I found was an area with a TV set where there was a coffee pot and a couch where an old guy was drinking coffee. Not my idea of a lounge.

I went to the front desk and asked the guy where their lounge was.

"Sorry," he answered. "We don't have a lounge, but there is one across the street at the Hilton."

"Thanks," I told him.

I walked outside and took a look up and down the street. There was a convenience store on the corner about a half block away and a pawn shop was about a half block up from that. There were no bars within eyesight.

I didn't really want to go over to the Hilton's lounge, but I didn't really want to go back to the room either. I went to the Hilton and followed an arrow that was labeled lounge.

*   *   *

I saw her the moment I walked into the darkened room. She was a tall woman, somewhere around five-feet-nine inches. She had a swagger in her attitude and her posture that said she was no stranger to lounges. She knew who she was and she knew what she had to offer.

She had a lot to offer.

She had long blond hair, golden curly ringlets that cascaded down around her shoulders. I wondered if she was a true blond or just a peroxide imitation. Only time would tell. She was wearing a form fitting, sparkling, short

156

silvery slick dress. The neckline hugged her throat like a choker. The dress shimmered as she stood at the bar. It showed off every curve of her figure. Her dress was just barely longer than a mini. Her legs were silky smooth with the right kind of hint of hard muscle. That dress- it hugged her body and her ass just the right way. It was so tight I could barely breathe.

I figured the direct approach was the best one. So I walked right up to the woman where she was leaning on the bar.

"Can I buy you a drink?" I asked.

"As long as it's a double rum and coke," she answered.

I ordered our drinks and took a good long close look at this woman.

She saw me looking and said, "Do you like?"

I noticed her voice was low and sultry, very sexy.

"Yes," I answered.

"Good," she said. "I wasn't always this pretty. I had to work real hard to get this way. For some of us, beauty is not a natural born gift."

"Your work definitely paid off," I told her and gave her another up and down look that she visibly appreciated.

"You can call me Robin," the woman told me and offered me her fingers to be kissed.

I did kiss them and noticed she had some muscle on those long fingers. This girl really did work to get the look that she had.

"You can call me Joe," I told Robin. I had no intention of telling anyone my real name in this city.

Robin didn't want to talk about herself, so we talked about me, or at least the story I made up about myself. For this trip, I was going to be an insurance salesman for Allstate and I didn't talk shop when I wasn't working. Since I didn't know anything about insurance this seemed to be a good way to handle the conversation.

With both of us being mysterious about our lives we had quite a few long silent pauses in our conversation. We spent these times looking each other over. The way Robin looked up and down my body made me feel like a juicy pork steak and my pork sausage was starting to heat up.

There was a piano man who played slow tunes and didn't sing too much at all.

We danced to the piano music and Robin hung on to me like a hungry octopus. She rubbed herself all over me and every curve and every inch of her was alive and squirming in my hands. She was like a big sexy anaconda snake who wanted to fold me in her coils and squeeze.

When the music finished, Robin kissed me deep and long. The power of that kiss almost took my breath away. She reached down and grabbed me, "You do like me, don't you," she said.

"Of course I do," I answered. "Come back to my room with me," I told her. "I'll show you how much."

She laughed and lightly punched me on the chest, "You are a very bad boy," she said and slipped her room key into my pocket. "I'm busy tonight, "Robin said." But come by tomorrow night and we'll be very bad together."

With that, she turned away from me and walked to the door of the lounge making a very elegant exit.

* * *

That night I dreamed about a woman in a shimmering dress. I dreamed of what was beneath that dress. A luscious perfect body. When I tried to make love to her, Robin started laughing at me.

I woke up in confusion with my heart pounding and covered in a cold sweat and I didn't have a clue as to why.

Well, you just never know about women. You just never know.

CHAPTER 38
PREPARATIONS

The next morning I had a taxi take me to one of the poorer sections of town where there was a string of pawn shops on the street. I went in a few of the pawn shops and took a look at the prices on some of their handguns.

I wanted the right price on a small handgun and I wanted the right person to buy it from. I'd know him when I saw him.

At the fifth pawn shop I entered, I saw him.

This is the guy the nickname *Weasel* was created for. He was small skinny and greasy. The thin black hair on his head was glued to his skull by sweat and oil. His skin was dark and oily. This guy gave off body odor like a cloud of noxious fumes. If this guy ever made it to a hot shower he'd probably melt and go right down the drain.

I was looking at the guns inside a locked glass counter when the weasel man came over. His body odor almost made my eyes water.

"Y'all wanta see somethin in there buddy," he said with a thick Georgia accent.

There was a chrome plated Forty-Five in the display case. It was a little bit worn but the gun looked like it would fire all right.

"I'll take a look at that one," I said and pointed at the Forty-Five.

The weasel brought the gun out and set it on the counter.

I picked the pistol up, made sure it wasn't loaded, then dry fired it a couple of times. The gun wasn't new, but it was in good working order.

I looked at the price tag: $150.00. The price was right.

"I'll take this one," I said.

The weasel brought out a form and laid it on the counter. "There's a waiting period," he said. "Ya got to fill out this here form."

I looked down at the form then back up to the weasel's face. "I don't have time to wait. I'm leaving town in two days."

"Well, I could be persuaded to back date that form," the weasel said. Then he smiled a wicked looking smile. "For a price."

"How much?" I asked.

"Let's call it a fifty dollar processing fee," the weasel said and grinned.

I pulled out a wad of bills from my pocket and counted out two hundred dollars.

I handed the weasel the money and put the pistol in my pocket.

The weasel snatched it up the form from the countertop. "I'll take care of this," he said. "Those forms are for everyone else. The government don't need to know who I sell to."

"That's right," I said and started toward the door.

"Hey," the weasel said as I reached the door. "You all ain't gonna go kill someone tonight are ya?"

I looked back at him and said, "You never can tell."

His laugh followed me out into the street.

*　　*　　*

I bought some bullets for the gun and a pair of work gloves at another store and spent the day walking around the neighborhood. It was warm here and green even in the wintertime. In East St. Louis everything seems to die around the middle of November. A drab grayness takes over the landscape that seems to seep inside your brain. After a while the winters in East St. Louis seem like living in a cemetery. The living vibrant blooming things of summer are just a memory out of the distant past.

Here the plants were still alive, the grass was still green. I could get used to living here, I thought. In this place everything didn't die once a year.

I felt the key that was still in my pocket.

That was a woman who was definitely alive and in bloom. She was vibrant. I might go and see her tonight.

Then I felt the chrome plated Forty-Five in my other pocket. Death was following me; or rather I was bringing him with me. Death was all around me, even in this green place. Death was a major part of my life.

No sense in me daydreaming of living somewhere other than where I did. What would I do, flip burgers in McDonalds? No, I was good at what I did.

The only skill necessary was the ability to turn off the switch and not feel anything.

I did that real well.

* * *

At three o'clock in the afternoon I took a dip in the hotel's pool. The water was ice cold and people looked at me like I was crazy. Maybe I was.

I knew the water was going to be cold before I ever jumped in. I guess I just wanted something to put me back into the mindset of what I had to do. This icy water helped me shut down my senses and made me feel cold all the way to my heart. I needed to feel cold inside.

The rest of the afternoon I spent making a homemade silencer for the Forty-Five. I did this by taking a plastic coke bottle and punching holes all over it with an ink pen. I cut a hole in the bottom large enough for the bullet to travel through unimpeded. Then I wrapped a dishtowel around the bottle and duct taped it in place.

The silencer was bulky but I'd keep a jacket wrapped around it until I was ready to use it.

* * *

Until about eight o'clock I watched what TV there was to watch in my room. Then I took a walk down the street to a pay phone.

I thought about walking to the Hilton and visiting Robin. But, no, I thought. I better get my business done as soon as possible. If I let myself think about something other than the job I was hired to do, then I could make mistakes.

If you make a mistake in this business, you can end up dead.

I dialed the Hilton Hotel desk and changed my voice as much as I could to a Boston accent.

The desk clerk answered, "Atlanta Hilton."

"I'm supposed to meet a friend of mine, Robert Perry, in one of your room's tomorrow morning. He gave me the number but I seem to have lost it." My Boston accent wouldn't fool a drama couch but I was just wanting to be unrecognizable.

"Hold on one moment," the desk clerk said. "I'll get it for you."

There was a moment of silence and the thought ran through my head, what if he wasn't checked into this hotel? What then? I could have made this phone call from St. Louis and saved myself the plane ride.

He came back to the phone then, "Robert Perry would be in room 512," he said.

"Thank you very much," I said and hung up.

CHAPTER 39
IN THE ROOM

At ten o'clock I walked across the street to the Atlanta Hilton. I was carrying the chrome forty-five with the silencer on it. I had my jacket draped over it. I was hoping that I looked like someone who was just too hot and was carrying his jacket.

I kept fingering the key to Robin's room as I walked to the Atlanta Hilton.

Maybe I'd go visit Robin if I got the job done quick, I said to myself.

Then I immediately thought that would really be smart. I could be in another room with my pants off when the body was found. Anyway, how was I going to explain showing up at her door with a gun equipped with a homemade silencer. "Hey, darlin, this is what helps me be sociable." That would go over real smooth.

I walked through the lobby and past the desk clerk making certain I made eye contact with no one. In the elevator alone, I pressed for the fifth floor and was relieved that no one got on at any other floor before I reached the fifth.

As I got off the elevator at the fifth floor, two large men got on the elevator. Both of them were grim faced with dead eyes and were wearing identical black dress suits and black shoes. These guys were obvious government agents.

I didn't care. There were headed in the other direction.

The hallway of the fifth floor was deserted.

Seven doors down was door 512.

I could hear televisions, talking, and laughing through the doors as I walked to 512.

I stopped in front of 512 and rapped lightly on it with the knuckles of my left hand.

I listened for any kind of a noise from the other side of the door.

There was only silence.

The story I was planning on telling if I had any problems getting the door open was that I had a cablegram for Robert Perry and it had to be signed for. Then I'd push my way inside and do the job. If anyone else was inside, well they'd have to go.

But no one was answering the door.

I knocked again, a little louder this time. No answer.

The elevator door opened. A fat man with his fat wife and two skinny kids got out of the elevator. Guess I knew where the food went to in that family.

They walked toward me.

I turned my back on them and pulled Robin's key out of my pocket. I was acting like I was trying to fit it into the lock when the door label attached to the key caught my eye.

The door number on it was 512.

My mind went a blank and I fitted the key into the lock.

What if she's inside, my mind screamed in silence. Could I pull the trigger on her? Could I?

How could she have given me this key?

The family stopped at the door directly across the hall from me. The man fidgeted in his pocket for his key. The kids were punching each other on the arms. Then they looked directly at me.

I turned the key and stepped through the door.

*   *   *

The lighting was dim. The only illumination in the room was a reading lamp at a desk. I looked around the darkened room and there was enough light for me to see that someone had already done my job for me.

The king size bed was a tangle of bloody sheets. There was someone in the bed who looked more like a carved up bloody side of beef than a man. I could tell it was a man though by the shape of the head and the blood covered torso. The man's face had deep slices across the cheeks. It looked

164

almost like the guy had fish gills. As I looked at the guy on the bed, I felt a strange familiarity.

I took the photo of Robert Perry out of my pocket. I leaned close to the blood soaked corpse on the bed.

Even through the coating of clotted blood on the man's face, I saw that this was Perry. This close to the brutalized body in front of me, that strange feeling of familiarity was much stronger.

I felt like I'd seen this man before, but I just couldn't figure out where or when.

I backed away from the carnage on the bed.

Nash was going to pay me for this kill, whether I'd done it or not. I could make up a story. He'd love to hear about how much this guy had suffered.

A square of white under the light on the desk caught my eye. A piece of ordinary writing paper. Something was written on it.

I listened for a moment for any sound. The unexpected finding of my intended victim, already dead and butchered, put me on edge. All I heard was the dripping of a faucet from the bathroom. The steady slow drip sounded loud in the silent room. The drip made a splashing sound, like water into water.

I glanced toward the bathroom. The door was closed, but a light shone from underneath it.

Someone might be in there.

Walking toward the bathroom I noticed my nose was burning. The air was thick and smoke was hanging in the air. The smell in the room was strangely familiar. I wasn't quite sure where I had smelled this burning smoke before, but I had.

Glancing around the room I saw that there was a pile of green leaves in a large ashtray. Smoke was curling up from the pile of leaves and making the musty stinging odor.

I took my jacket off my arm and laid it across the back of a chair and put my pair of working gloves on. I hadn't touched anything yet, but I wasn't going to take any chances with forgetting and laying my hand on something and leaving my prints behind.

There wasn't any reason to keep concealing the Forty-Five in a room with a chopped up dead man on the bed. It was a sure bet that if I met someone in the bathroom they were not going to be friendly.

I was having an intense sense of Deja Vu as I approached the bathroom. With the subdued lighting and the heavy stinging smoke in the air mingled with the smell of the blood from the guy on the bed, I almost felt like I was back in Tor Ambrose's house.

It wasn't possible that Tor had set this up.

He was dead. Julia had seen to that by putting that bullet in his forehead.

I turned the knob on the bathroom door and pushed the door open. The white tiles on the walls combination shower bath were streaked with red.

The tub was filled with water to overflowing. The water was bright red. A man's body was submerged in the water. It looked like he had the same kind of slices on his face as the man on the bed. The smell of blood and death was heavy in the bathroom. Blood was all over the floor and the sink. So I guessed that he had been killed then placed in the tub.

I went back out into the other room. My thought was that I had better get the hell out of here. As I crossed the room to collect my jacket the square of white under the desk lamp caught my eye again.

The note on the table was written to me.

> Mr. Dark,
> I know where you have been.
> I know where you are.
> I know where you will be.
> You cannot hide from me.
> I will be coming for you.

The letter was unsigned and it made a chill run down my back.

Just what the hell was going on here?

I folded the note up and put it in my pocket. I didn't want my name left in this room.

Just out of the circle of lamps light on the desk was a wig. A blond wig. A long blond wig made of golden curly ringlets.

I looked at the wig, then I looked at Robert Perry bloody and dead on the bed.

No way in hell that could be, I thought.

I walked to the closet and looked at the clothes that were hung up. There were two men's shirts, two pair of men's slacks and there were two women's dresses. One of the dresses was a short sparkling silvery dress.

That's just great, I thought. The woman I've been lusting after for the last day isn't even a woman. Robert Perry is Robin.

The vision of how I must have looked kissing Robin flashed through my mind. My stomach felt strangely queasy.

I knew I had to leave that room and fast.

CHAPTER 40
GOING BACK

Back in my hotel room I took the silencer off the Forty-Five and cut it up into pieces with my pocket knife. That went into the trash can. Then I opened the window and tossed the Forty-Five into the alley behind the hotel.

After calling a taxi to take me to the airport I sat down and thought about the confusing events of that night. I tried to puzzle out what it all could mean and gave up when the knock came on the door. There didn't seem to be any sense to what had happened. But life never did seem to make sense anyway.

My cab driver was a short fat guy with a Brooklyn accent. I talked to him on the way to the airport and he was friendly enough to answer back when he wasn't dodging the other cars.

I made up a story about wandering into a cross dresser's stage show downtown and asked him what he thought about them.

"Those guys scare the hell out of me," he blurted out. "I was visiting some of my wife's relatives in Nashville and her brothers talked me into seein' a show with them called *Maybe Dames*. One of em was dressed up like Marilyn Monroe. One of em was dressed like Diana Ross and you know all of em was lookin like these famous chics. Well, that was OK. I was havin a good time sayin things like, you know, these chicks really got balls. That was until the one that looked like Gina Lollobrigida walked out."

"I've had the hots for her since I was like five years old. She's the one that gave me my first hard-on back when I thought all my dick was for was waterin' weeds. Right then I got a stiffy I could have broken the table in half with. And ya know what, no matter how many times I told myself that that chick had the same equipment that Arnold Schwarzenegger has, I couldn't get rid of that hard on."

"I was glad the place was dark. If one of my brother-in-laws had a said somethin' I'd of kicked his ass right then and there. That was a very confusing night. So I don't go nowhere near those kinda shows no more."

My night had been confusing too. The more I thought about it the more confused I got.

*　　*　　*

On the plane back to St. Louis I finished up reading, *Hard Road Ahead* and tried to take a nap. I couldn't even come close to sleep.

The image of Robin kept popping into my head. The image kept being superimposed with how Robert Perry had looked on the bed with blood all over his head from having his face sliced open like it had been. Then I'd see the picture that Graham had given me and I'd wonder how in hell I couldn't see Robert Perry even through the makeup, dress, and wig.

My mind wandered around in the darkness behind my eyes.

I found myself driving down a desolate two lane highway. I was driving a red Fifty-Seven Chevy Convertible. A brunette was in the seat beside me. She was smiling and laughing wildly. I looked at her directly in the eyes.

Her eyes were dark, wicked looking eyes.

"Well Max," she said in a mocking tone of voice. "You just can't tell about women can you?"

She reached over and undid my fly with her hand and took my dick out. She stroked me and made me hard and was giggling in an evil way the whole time.

I realized I was the guy from the novel I'd just finished reading and this woman was June, the wayward conniving wife.

"Hey Max," June said pumping my dick furiously. "Do you really want to know about women?"

"Oh yeah," I told her and she jammed her head down on my dick and sucked me viciously. It felt incredibly good.

Then she stopped and lifted her head from my crotch with a final sound like a plunger being pulled from a toilet.

The face that came up and stared at me dripping blood all over my crotch was Robert Perry's sliced up face.

"There's nothing to know," Perry said and ripped the wig off and threw it out of the speeding car. "You never can tell about women," he screamed at me. "You never can tell!"

I woke up so violently, I kicked and punched the seat in front of me.

The stewardess announced we would begin the approach to Lambert Airport shortly.

I was really happy we were going to be on the ground.

* * *

By the time I got my car from the long term parking lot it was starting to get light outside. The eastern sky was turning to rusty red and traffic was starting to pick up. I took I-270 back to the bridge over to East St. Louis. Then it was back to my apartment where I left a message for Graham Nash to call me when he got in.

I was hungry and tired. More tired than hungry so I laid down to take a nap for a few hours. On the way to my bed I grabbed a bottle of Wild Turkey whiskey and took a deep pull from it. It made me gag and took my breath away.

That was some horrible tasting shit, I thought. I was going to have to think about giving this stuff up.

Then I took another drink and it went down smoother the second time. Even though it did still burn like hell. The liquor hit my brain and that wonderful dizziness overtook me. Well, maybe I would rethink this quitting business.

* * *

The ringing of the phone was driving nails into my brain. I woke from a dreamless sleep and was grateful for the lack of dreams.

The gravelly voice on the line was Graham Nash. "We have to talk," he said immediately.

"You're right about that," I said. "I need to get paid."

His laugh came loud through the phone. "Right," he said laughing. "Meet me at Roxie's as soon as you can get there." He hung up.

I was getting dressed and still wondering what Graham's laughing was about when a knock came at the door.

I put on my holster and Thirty-Eight and I answered the door. Rosa Delgado walked into the room. That was when I remembered that it was her day to come and do the weekly cleaning that I paid her for.

She wrinkled up her nose and glanced around the apartment, "Whooo," she said. "Something stinks here."

I couldn't smell anything. I told her, "You always tell me something stinks here."

"And something always does, but today it is worse." She walked around the apartment looking behind things until she went in the bathroom.

She yelled, "Iiieeechee, Mi Madre!" She came out of the bathroom holding her nose and fanning the air in front of her face.

"What?" I asked.

"I'm not cleaning that up," she said.

I went in the bathroom and remembered the mess I'd left in the toilet a couple days earlier. The odor was incredible.

I came out of the bathroom holding my nose too. My eyes were burning and I was gagging.

I was met just outside the door by Rosa.

She was holding out a plunger to me that she got from my closet. She had a stern look on her face. She pushed the plunger into by hands.

"You get back in there and clean that up," she commanded me.

I waved her away and said, "Hey I gotta get some air."

She followed me to the window. I opened the window and stuck my head out of it. I sucked in what clean air I could get. There isn't too much of that in East St. Louis. Then I pulled my head back into the room.

Rose was straightening up around the place. She saw me back inside the room and breathing well.

She pointed at the bathroom. "Get to work!" She demanded.

"You're a cruel woman," I told her and headed back to the bathroom.

Rosa shook her finger at me and said, "I have to be to keep you in line."

So I went into the bathroom with my plunger and did battle with the beast I'd created.

CHAPTER 41
JUNKIES AND PHOTOS

I picked up a Whopper at the Burger King drive through and ate it on the way to Roxie's.

Sometimes a fast food burger shop is like a gift from God. Before I had that, I was so hungry I would've eaten anything that wasn't running fast.

Anybody that doesn't think America is a great country should spend a year and a half in the jungle of Viet Nam. That will make you appreciate a Whopper in a new way.

It was around 1:00 PM when I got to Roxie's. Their parking lot was almost empty. They didn't have their big neon sign lit today. From the outside of Roxie's the only light on was a small open sign. The windows were blacked out. They didn't want anyone to get a free show.

I walked in and was not charged a cover charge. There was no show going on. There was only a barely clothed barmaid and a barely clothed waitress working in the dimly lit club. The club's bouncer was snoring in a chair in a corner.

Graham Nash was sitting at the bar drinking a mixed drink. Graham downed his drink in one gulp and met me in the middle of the floor. He motioned me to follow him outside and we walked to his car together.

Old newspaper and trash blew across the parking lot. The wind was cold and heavy gray snow clouds hung low in the sky. This cold day in East St. Louis was definitely a change from Atlanta.

Graham looked like any ordinary middle aged businessman in his gray leisure suit as he walked across the parking lot. As he approached his car, a Lincoln Continental, a scraggly looking, skinny black crack addict stepped into his path.

The junky made a crazy looking face, bearing his teeth and bulging his eyes out. The guy was breathing heavy and he stunk like a roast left out in the sun too long.

"Motherfucker," he wheezed, looking in Graham's eyes like he belonged in The State Mental Hospital. "White boy, gimme all you got." He held a rusty looking pocket knife in his hand.

Graham glanced at me with the bored look that some people would use when inconvenienced by a rude child.

"Sure thing," he said calmly and reached inside his inside coat pocket.

The junky was making little gimme gestures with his left hand in front of Graham's face.

Graham jerked a small chrome derringer from under his coat and stuck it to the addict's forehead.

The junky flung his hands out to the sides of his head and dropped the knife. "Don't kill me man," he wailed. "Oh man, please don't fuckin kill me."

Graham said, "You mean you don't want this?"

The junky sank down to his knees in front of Graham. He was whining like a spanked puppy. "Oh, don't, don't shoot me, don't!"

Quietly Graham whispered, "Get the fuck out of here."

The junky scuttled away from us on all fours.

We got in Graham's car. He made a circle around the parking lot to where the junky was walking along the edge of the pavement.

Graham swerved at him and made him jump into a ditch that was full of stagnant water. The junkie landed with a splash and sank up to his waist.

Graham laughed then glanced at me and said, "I love this neighborhood. It's so classy."

While he was driving east on Madison Avenue, Graham reached into his left shirt jacket pocket.

"I know it wasn't you that killed Robert Perry," he said and dropped two folded up sheets of paper on the seat next to me. "These are the two guys that did."

I picked up the sheets of paper and unfolded them. Graham kept speaking as I studied the sheets of paper that had been faxed to him.

The two sheets were photos of people.

Graham said, "The Atlanta DEA's office has been keeping the Hilton under surveillance for quite some time because of drug deals going down there. They were watching the guy that went to Perry's room. These two went in after him and were never seen leaving. Our guys went in with a pass key to bust them but the party was already over. You saw what they saw. They left to bring in the local cops when you were arriving."

I looked at the two faxed photos hard and then looked at Graham.

"You know who they are, don't you?" I said.

"Of course I know who they are," Graham said. He pulled off Madison Avenue into the parking lot of a Target store. He parked in one of the far corners away from any of the other cars.

"These photos were taken by a hidden camera just outside of Perry's room at about seven o'clock last night," Graham said. "We both know for a fact that these two men were dead over three months ago."

He was right. We both did know that these two men were already dead. The photos were of Morris West and Tor Ambrose.

CHAPTER 42
DEAD MEN

What do you make of all this?" I asked Graham and indicated the photos.

"I was hoping you would have some answers," he said. "Since you don't, I'm taking us to the city morgue. I want to know what happened to their bodies."

That was something I wanted to know too.

I took a good closer look at the pictures of Tor Ambrose and Morris West and what I saw didn't make me feel any better.

Both were wearing hats but there was no mistaking who they were.

The photos weren't exceptionally clear, but the one of Tor Ambrose was clear enough to show that his hair was singed and his skin had the slick look of a burn victim. I'd done that by throwing a few lit oil lamps in his face.

The pictures of Morris West were even more disturbing. His forehead was slightly caved in and I could see signs of stitch marks. Well, I thought, the guy who stitched his head back together didn't know what Morris looked like before he arrived on his table at the morgue. When I put my Thirty-Eight to his forehead and pulled the trigger, that's what caved in his forehead. Morris West still showed the signs of that shot.

According to this picture, he was still up and walking around, when he couldn't possibly be doing that.

Both of these guys showed the marks of what I did to them. If they were really out and strolling around, it was a sure bet they would be looking for some pay back.

*   *   *

When we arrived at the East St. Louis City Morgue, Graham took us down to the basement where they stored the bodies and the records. We went through some heavy swinging wood doors into a white room lit by glaring florescent lamps.

Along one wall was what looked like rows of small lockers with handles on them. On the other wall were filing cabinets and a desk with a man sitting at it doing paperwork and drinking coffee. There was a surgical table in the middle of the room and surgical supplies on smaller tables around it.

From the way the man looked at us by snapping his head around when we walked in, I could tell this guy was definitely the nervous type.

Graham walked right to the guy and I followed. The guy at the desk looked like he got jittery with each step we took toward him.

"We need to know what happened to two bodies you had here," Graham told the guy with the long neck and white uniform. He wore a name tag that read, Charles.

"Why, yes, yes of course," he answered stammering, "If I can help at all, I certainly will."

I took the faxed photos out of my pocket and handed them to Charles. He looked at the photos and if it could have been possible, he seemed to get even paler than he already was.

Charles quickly glanced around the room. He grabbed his coffee and took a big drink of it.

He shoved the photos back at us.

"I, I, I, don't know anything about them," he said.

Graham wasn't having any of that. He flipped out his DEA badge at the dead body clerk and told him, "We didn't even give you their names. The way you reacted to those pictures, I know you remember them. Tell me what happened or I'll bring you up on charges."

This wasn't the kind of guy who could take much pressuring so I wasn't surprised when he cracked wide open right then.

"Look," he said. "It wasn't my fault. I can't explain what happened that day. These two guys. I'll never forget them. I haven't slept too much since they were here. They were supposed to go to Barnes Hospital for the medical students to carve up since they had no known next of kin and no one wanted to claim their bodies.

"The day before they're set to be shipped to Barnes, a guy showed up and asks where they are. I pointed out their drawers and showed him their bodies." Charles pointed to two of the lockers. "When I showed him the bodies he touched each of them once on the forehead and I swear I thought I was seeing things, but I thought I saw both of them take in a deep breath when he touched them.

"When he was doing it I felt like I couldn't move. It was like I was froze or something. I was like that until he left. After he left I closed the drawers up. I got to admit, I was kind of shook up by what I'd seen. What really shook me up though was about ten minutes later when the banging started coming from inside those drawers.

"Those two guys were trying to get out.

"I ran out to go get the guard from upstairs. When we got back the drawers were open and the two bodies were gone."

Graham said to Charles, "You're trying to tell me that you had two dead bodies that got up and walked out?"

Charles said, "I'm not trying to tell you anything. I just told you exactly what happened. My boss wasn't too happy either. Hey, if I didn't have a wife and kids to support I'd have quit right then. But I just can't afford it."

For some strange reason I believed every word that Charles was saying. I got the distinct feeling that he was too scared and too freaked out to be able to lie.

Graham asked Charles, "What did the guy look like that came in here and touched the bodies?"

"See, that is something that bothers me too," Charles answered. "I can't remember what he looked like at all. I've tried to remember, so I can give a description or something. But whenever I try to recall what he looks like, it's like I have a blank spot there."

Graham looked at me and I nodded my head. I'd heard this kind of thing before.

The coach of Felicia's chess team had been able to see the guy who he noticed was around the kids at their chess tournaments. That had been Tor Ambrose. He had even been able to give me a description of Tor, even if it had been very vague.

Whenever he tried to approach Tor to ask him why he was hanging around the kids, well he would just seemingly vanish.

What this guy was telling us was different, yet in a strange way it was the same. He could remember what the guy had done and that he had spoken to him but he couldn't get a picture of the guy in his mind.

It was almost like that part of Charles' mind has been blocked.

Graham handed Charles his card. He told him, "If that guy comes back again, you give me a call immediately."

"You don't have to worry about that," Charles said, "If he comes back I'm calling you, the police, and anyone else I can get down here quick."

*   *   *

Graham drove me back to Roxie's where my car was. On the way I told him, "Don't expect to get back that thirty seven hundred dollars you paid me."

He laughed about that. "I'm calling that a retainer for future services. I'm sure you'll be there when I need you in the future."

"As long as you got the cash," I told him.

"It's never my cash anyway," he said. "It's always company funds."

Then Graham surprised me. He came out with the kind of explanation that he never would have before.

"This Robert Perry," he said, "was more personal than business. I knew Perry through informants. Perry and his queens took over Tor Ambrose's territory when you took Tor out of the picture. We couldn't nail Perry. He seemed to always know whenever we got information that his shipments were coming in. He'd change his plans and we'd end up busting an empty barge on the river or an empty tractor trailer."

I listened to him speak in silence.

Graham said, "Until my son committed suicide and left me a note, I couldn't figure out how Perry was always one step ahead of me. My son's note said that Perry had been blackmailing him for information he got from me. Robert Perry was such a good female impersonator that my son Don

179

never even knew he was having an affair with a man until he was being blackmailed. Don had a wife and kids. It messed him up so bad he put a gun in his mouth and pulled the trigger."

"Well," I told Graham. "I may not have pulled the trigger on Perry but after what I saw was left of him, believe me, he died slow and in pain."

"I do suppose that is something," Graham said. "Now we have to deal with Tor, or what's left of him."

"Yeah," I told Graham. "But I get the feeling there's something a lot worse than Tor out there this time."

Graham said, "Me, too."

CHAPTER 43
DOWN MEMORY LANE

I left Roxie's and drove by Julia's but like I thought, neither she nor Felicia were home. It was still too early in the day. Julia was still at work and Felicia was still in school.

If Tor Ambrose was out roaming around, whether he was alive or dead, I thought Julia should be aware of it. That would now have to wait. I left a note on her door to call me.

Not knowing what else to do at that moment, I drove over to Johnny's place. On the way over to Johnny's the heavy gray clouds that had been threatening to drop buckets of snow on the city started doing just that. Heavy large snowflakes looking like feathers started pouring down from the sky.

Within about two minutes after the snow started I was using the windshield wipers. The snow was so thick that by the time I got to Johnny's the ice was building up on the sides and bottom of the windshield and it was getting hard to see. The weather was quickly beginning to look like a blizzard.

Maybe I should have stayed in Atlanta, I thought, as I got out of my car and trudged into Johnny's.

When I opened the door and snow blew in around me, Johnny yelled, "Man close that door. What's the matter with you. You born in a barn?"

I shut the door behind me, shook the snow off, and before my eyes could adjust to the gloom of the bar room, I heard a high pitched laughing coming from the table where Johnny and I usually played chess. When my eyes adjusted I saw that Johnny was behind the bar and a rather short woman with black coffee skin was sitting at the table in front of our chess board.

"I have beaten him again," the woman said and again laughed. She had a thick Cajun accent. Her words were a little hard to understand, but she spoke like she was giving a speech by projecting her words. "Do you wish for me to beat you now?" She said and laughed with a childish playfulness in her voice.

I was finding myself liking this woman already.

"I see you've met Grandma Jeanette," Johnny said from behind the bar. "Do you want a beer?"

"Always," I told Johnny and sat down across the board from Jeanette.

"John, John!" Jeanette said forcefully to Johnny. "Do not call me Grandma. Only call me Jeanette. I am too young to be called Grandma. Do I look like a toothless old woman to you?"

"Sorry Gra… uh Jeanette," Johnny said. "But you are my Grandma. Why don't you want me to call you that?"

"I do not like the name Ma," Jeanette said. "It sounds like a noise a cow would make. I am that which I wish to be and I do not wish to be a noise a cow would make. You may call be Grand or Jeanette or Grand Jeanette but do not call me Grandma. I will not answer to it."

I laughed and Jeanette smiled at me. She seemed to look quite a bit younger than she could possibly be. When she smiled Jeanette's face positively glowed.

"You put him in his place," I told Jeanette.

"Fuck you," Johnny said from behind the bar.

I sat down across from Jeanette and Johnny came with two beers.

"And what about me?" Jeanette said to Johnny.

Johnny and me looked at each other.

"I do not want a beer," Jeanette said. "I want a shot of the strongest whiskey you have."

Johnny started to go behind the bar and stopped. He asked, "Are you sure you want my strongest whiskey? I've got some white lightning that'll melt paint."

Jeanette said, "Maybe too strong for you, but not for me."

We set the pieces up for a new game and Johnny brought Jeanette a shot from the bottle of white lightening he had under the bar. When Johnny sat down at the table Jeanette pointed at me.

"You are also John," she said. "There are too many Johns here. What shall I call you to differentiate you from my grandson?"

"We do look almost like twins," I told Jeanette and I leaned my head toward Johnny and he leaned toward me. We both grinned at Jeanette.

"Can you tell us apart?" Johnny asked his Grandmother.

"I should slap you both," she said, "For acting the fool."

I had the white pieces on my side so I moved my queen's pawn out two squares.

Jeanette picked up the shot of white lightening and slugged it down in one quick swallow. She let out an "Ahhhhh."

We were both watching her intently. I knew for a fact Johnny's white lightening would take my breath away because it burned like lit gasoline.

She smiled at us. "Too weak," she said and moved her queen's pawn out two spaces.

Playing Jeanette was no contest at all. She basically beat the hell out of me. We played two games in under an hour and she just toyed with me.

During our games, Jeanette started calling me J.D., which was all right with me. Jeanette showed up at Johnny's unexpectedly about two hours before I had shown up. She was definitely a very interesting woman. She looked to be in her early fifties. When I made a comment on her looking so young she proudly announced that she was ninety-one years old.

My mouth must have just about hit the floor when she told me that from the way she laughed at my reaction. "My God, you look like you could be Johnny's sister," I told her truthfully.

"Yes," she said. "I believe I am young and so I am."

I couldn't argue with a philosophy with results like that.

*   *   *

The snow was coming down in buckets. It reminded me of when I was a kid and we first moved to East St. Louis. My dad had been a cop in Crystal City, Missouri. He was working the night my mother was killed in a robbery at a grocery store.

My dad hadn't been the cuddliest father on the block even before my mom died; afterward he was ten times worse.

I think that maybe my mom had been a release valve for my dad's anger. I could remember some yelling coming from their bedroom at night and I had seen a few bruises on my mom, but if my dad had hit my mom I never actually witnessed it. After my mom was gone, my dad started drinking heavily.

He would yell at me and take a swing at me whenever he would get the chance. I had an older brother that he drove out of the house and into the army when he was sixteen. My brother was killed in Viet Nam.

My dad was booted off the Crystal City Police Department after repeated instances of beating handcuffed prisoners. When my dad went job hunting most of the police departments turned him away.

When my dad applied to the East St. Louis Police Department he found out they were looking for the same kind of cop that he was. He was brutal and mean and that was what a cop in East St. Louis needed to be to survive.

The day that I was remembering was cold as hell and snowing buckets. It was my first day of school at Washington Junior High.

I had been frozen stiff with fear when the teacher introduced me to the class. I looked out from her desk at a sea of black and brown and yellow faces. I was the only white in the school.

I was about thirteen years old on that first school day at Washington Junior High. At the end of home room I had my first experience with being beaten up by a group of kids before I even got to my first class. Those kids didn't need a reason to kick the shit out of me. I was just new and a different color than they were, so they just beat the hell out of me. That is just the way it was.

At that school I was alone and friendless. When the bell rang that ended one class, I'd run and dodge the other kids as fast as I could. If I didn't, I'd make it to my next class bruised up and bloodied.

That went on for about two weeks and either I was slowing down or the other kids had figured out my routes from one class to the next. Whatever it was, I took a beating in between every class the last couple days of the second week.

Complaining to my dad made no sense. He gave me a beating whenever I came home with any marks on me at all. I came home marked up every day. So I got a beating at home every day.

The Saturday after I'd had a particularly bad Friday by getting kicked down the stairs, a knock came on my front door about ten in the morning. I looked out the front window and saw three black kids, one Mexican kid and one Oriental kid waiting for me on the porch.

It was snowing heavily on them and they all looked cold breathing steam out there. This group of kids looked like they were a couple of years older than me. So I expected to get a worse beating than usual.

They knocked on the door again and my dad yelled from his bedroom, "Answer that damn door or I'll come out there and ram your head through it."

I was stuck between a rock and a hard place. Actually I was stuck between a beating and a worse beating. I figured I'd probably survive the beating from the kids outside. My Dad had gotten so drunk the night before that I knew he'd have a bad hangover. I wasn't so sure I would survive the beating he'd give me.

I turned the knob and stepped outside into the wind and the stinging snow.

The leader of the small gang was a big black kid. He would grow up to be much bigger before he was done growing. His name was Joe Briggs. Now, years later, he's a cop that hates me with a passion.

He looked me up and down and said, "I've been seein' you have trouble at school."

I had my fists doubled up because I figured trouble had just followed me home.

"It ain't nothing I can't handle," I told him.

"The way your head bounced down those steps yesterday, I think you do need our help," he said.

"Look man," another one of the black guys who was to become my best friend, Johnny Davis, said. "We're offering to let you hang with us. You'd be crazy not to."

"I can handle myself," I told them.

Joe Briggs looked at me hard. "Before you go mistrustin' us because we a bunch of Negroes," he said. "Understand this, they don't pick on you cause you're white, they pick on you cause you're alone and can't do a damn thing about it."

The Mexican kid spoke up now. I forget his name because he's been dead a long time. He said, "Fuck this guy man. He wants to keep getting his ass wasted, that's fine by me. We don't need that little fuckhead with us no how." He turned and started to walk away and the others started to turn away. "And who you callin Negro anyway?" He asked Joe Briggs. "I am Hispanic."

"I'm callin me and my two brother's Negroes and we're proud of it," Joe told him. "You was callin' yourself a spic before I told you to have some self-respect and stop doin' that."

"Hey, wait a minute," I asked the group. "Where you guys headin' to?"

"We're just walking around," the Oriental kid said. I later found out his name was Ben Lee. He's still a good friend of mine and he owns a restaurant that serves the best curry in existence.

Johnny spoke up then, "We'll probably end up at the Southside Community Center and shoot some pool."

"Hold on a second," I told them. I reached inside the door and grabbed my coat off a hook. "I'll go with you."

I went with them and after freezing for a while on the streets and throwing snowballs at each other, we did go and shoot some pool.

On Monday morning when the five kids who normally beat me up showed up outside my homeroom, so did my new group of friends. The opposing gang backed down quickly when they saw that our guys were bigger than theirs.

The leader of the other gang told me he was going to get me later. So we faced off after school and slugged it out.

I won the fight only because I was so used to getting beaten on that he couldn't do anything to me by himself that could hurt me very much. He beat on my head until his hands were swollen and bloody. He couldn't hit me anymore because his hands were so sore, so I took over. I gave him a beating until he was on his hand and knees and was curled up into a ball on the ground.

Johnny walked with me to my home that night.

He told me, "You really are one tough son of a bitch. But if you don't learn how to fight the right way, someone is going to beat your brains out."

All I did was smile at him through my bloodied and smashed lips. It felt good to win for a change.

About a week later after my lumps shrunk down a little bit, Johnny took me to Pop O'Grady's Gymnasium to learn to box. After that, the only trouble I had in school was keeping from being sent to the reform school for beating up other kids.

CHAPTER 44
WARNINGS

I checked my watch again and saw that it was about the time that Julia and Felicia should be getting home.

Jeanette and Johnny were playing another game of chess. Jeanette was beating him without any effort. It was another triumph for women's lib, I thought.

"I'm gonna be taking off," I told them and stood up. "Got some business I gotta take care of."

Jeanette stood up and intensely looked into my face. "Tell Johnny about the dead men who walk," she said to me in a commanding voice. "That is why I am here and my grandson needs to know!"

Johnny looked at me. "What's my Grandma talkin about?"

Jeanette gave him a mean look and he said, "Sorry about the Grandma, Jeanette."

"Thank you," she answered.

I weighed the situation for a moment. Then I decided to tell Johnny and Jeanette the whole story about the Robert Perry job.

When I was done Johnny said to me, "Man you do get yourself into some shit don't you?"

"Even if Mr. Dark had not taken the job of murdering Robert Perry," Jeanette said. "Robert Perry and the other man in that room would have died just the same. They were both marked for early death a long time ago."

I looked into Jeanette's eyes intently and saw an extremely intelligent woman looking back. "If you don't mind me asking you this," I said to her. "How do you know so much about all of this?"

Johnny laughed and shook his head.

Jeanette smiled at me and said, "I have been a Houngan voodoo priestess my whole life, ever since I was a little girl. A Houngan is someone who sees and hears more than others. We can influence the world with what we know if we wish. I only wish a long and happy life and to protect my grandson."

I looked at Johnny and he said, "Jeanette's always known about things that were going to happen to people. She'd warn people if she could and sometimes they'd listen. When they didn't, bad things happened to them."

He looked at Jeanette. "Like I remember you told that guy not to take his family to Santa Rosa Island in Florida for vacation. The bridge collapsed from under his car on the way out to the island. His car and about ten others went into the gulf. His entire family drowned."

I asked Jeanette, "Ok, assuming you can see a bit of the future. What do you see about a Julia and Felicia Richardson?"

She smiled again at me and spoke slowly, "It does not work like that. This gift, or curse, that I have, is not like a phone book. I only know that there is one in this city who is a Bokor, a voodoo sorcerer and he is much much more. He is evil on a level that you cannot even comprehend. No one in this city is safe so long as he is here."

"I've got to go and warn Julia and Felicia," I told them. "If that bastard does anything to them, I'm gonna make him wish he was dead."

"He may not be as easy to kill as you would think," Jeanette told me. She reached into a large handbag that I now noticed was beside her and handed me a small bottle of what looked like water.

The bottle was about the size of an aspirin bottle. It may have been my imagination but I thought I saw the bottle glow a soft blue as I took it out of Jeanette's hand.

"This may help you against the dead who walk, if they truly are dead," she said.

"And what if they're not dead?" I asked her.

Jeanette smiled at me again, but her smile was strangely grim and foreboding. She said, "In that case, you are on your own."

PART II

THE CHILL
OF
DEATH

"It is my nature to sting you,"
Said the scorpion.
"I am what I am."
- From the Fable
"The Frog and The Scorpion"

"Good and Evil
In themselves
Are Passive Forces,
But once you move
Toward one
Then, you become
As a magnet."
- The Walker in Darkness

There are many more things
Than you or I could dream
And I have many nightmares
Many terrible, evil dreams.
- The Walker in Darkness

CHAPTER 45
PLAYING TAG WITH THE BOYS

In less than two hours it looked like the sky had dropped more than two feet of snow on the ground. The roads were rapidly becoming impassible. I was having to drive slowly down the road with my head stuck out of the window because my windshield wipers were practically useless. There was a layer of ice on the windshield that the wipers were riding on top of.

Most people were hiding in their houses today. Even the junkies and winos were off the streets. Usually they were so numbed out that no kind of weather bothered them at all. Today the weather was so severe that even they were trying to find shelter.

I was beginning to wonder if I was going completely out of my mind. If you had told me last week I was going to be warning someone that they had better go into hiding from a dead man out walking around, I'd have told you to go fuck yourself. But now, here I was on my way to do just that. Not only that, but it seems like I'd just picked up a sudden belief in voodoo.

What the hell is going on in my head, I asked myself and wiped the slush away that was accumulating on my forehead. Hell, I was even believing in Jeanette's ability to tell the future without questioning it at all.

All of this was beginning to have the feel of some kind of a weird LSD flashback. Except that the snow stinging my face felt all too real for this to be any kind of hallucination.

Before I'd left Johnny's place, I'd given him Graham Nash's number with instructions to call him and tell Graham where I was going if I didn't call him in two hours. In this weather, I didn't know if he could arrange any help anyway.

It was only about five o'clock in the afternoon but the sky was looking much darker than it should for this time of day. The clouds appeared grayer and heavier than any other snow clouds I can ever remember seeing. If I hadn't have known better, I could have sworn I saw a lightning flash from up in those clouds.

That was impossible of course.

Then I remembered what happened to Tor's house right after I interrupted his sacrificing Felicia to some pagan god.

I was so shell shocked the night Tor's house went up in splinters from a lightning bolt that I didn't even bat an eye at it. Now that I thought about it, maybe the timing for the lightning bolt hitting Tor's house was a little more than just circumstantial. Maybe Tor had pissed off someone other than me that night.

Then again, maybe I'd pissed off someone that night but their aim just wasn't too good. That was a nice thought.

*   *   *

My whole world was blanketed in thick white as I drove slowly down the streets toward Julia's house. Some kids were out on the streets throwing snowballs. The sound of their voices as they shouted to each other was muffled. Their shouts broken up by the snow sounded like loud whispering. With the snow showing white on their heads, shoulders and backs, the kids looked strangely like winter gremlins.

I turned the corner onto Julia's street and all was silence there. No one was out on this street. Everything was dead on this street except for Julia's house.

I brought my car to a sliding halt and jumped out the door. The front door to Julia's house had been ripped off the hinges and was laying in the bushes to the right of the door. I ran to the doorway slipping and sliding the whole way and nearly falling on the porch.

Julia's living room was an obstacle course of turned over and broken furniture. A sudden mental image of the bleeding and broken bodies of Julia and Felicia rushed through my mind. I had to force it away. That vision did make my heart stop cold in my chest just like I'd been hit there. I realized right then if anything had happened to Julia or Felicia I would kill whoever was involved.

I stepped over the shattered furniture and into the house. The wind whistled in after me and straight out the back door. I could see the back door open through the kitchen at the back of the house. The back door slammed shut when a burst of wind came screaming through.

The kitchen was wrecked just like the living room was. There were broken dishes and glasses littered all over the floor. The icebox was turned over on its face and the dining table was on its side.

I cupped my hands to my mouth and yelled Julia's and Felicia's names.

There was a moment of silence that seemed to stretch out like hours. Only the sound of the echo of my voice came back to me.

Then the sound of something heavy crashing to the floor came from where I knew Julia's bedroom was. Something smashed to the floor in Felicia's bedroom as well.

I went into the hallway that led into both of the bedrooms and both of the bedroom doors were jerked open simultaneously.

Into the hallway stepped two men who I'd never thought I'd see again. It was Tor Ambrose and Morris West, and neither of them were looking happy.

Both of them looked at me with dead eyes and their faces were grayish and expressionless.

They were moaning slightly and took a step toward me.

I jerked out my Thirty-Eight from my holster and took aim at Tor, the closest one to me.

"Hold it motherfucker," I yelled at him. "Or I'll put your ass back in the ground where you belong."

They both acted like they hadn't heard anything and came on toward me. They were both moving slowly, lurching forward like they were doing a bad impersonation of a Frankenstein monster.

"Where's Julia and Felicia?" I yelled at them. But they didn't seem interested in answering.

I knew I had to get past these two to see if Julia and Felicia were in their bedrooms and if they were alive.

Tor took another lurching step toward me and I pointed my Thirty-Eight at his face. I pulled the trigger twice and my gun roared in my fist. Tor was knocked backward. Holes were punched completely through his head. Blood and fragments of brain and bone sprayed all over the face of Morris West behind him. Tor stumbled backward and went down on his back in an ungainly heap.

I took aim at Morris West's face who stepped over Tor's body.

"You hold it motherfucker or you're next," I shouted at him. My ears were ringing from the sounds of the shots in the small hallway.

Morris came on and I saw behind him, to my horror that Tor sat up on the floor.

I fired three times into Morris West's head and his face was turned into a red ruin. He spun sideways, fell over Tor, and went down on his face on the floor.

Tor got to his feet now. A chill ran all the way through me when I looked at the deep holes in Tor's head. There was no way on earth that he could be on his feet and coming at me. But, that was just what he was doing. I holstered the empty Thirty-Eight.

The sight of Tor coming at me with his head hanging open and his brains exposed must have driven me a bit insane. I jumped forward and yelled something like, "You need to be dead, you sack of shit," and kicked him as hard as I could in the balls with my left foot and drove a hard right cross through his jaw.

I thought the punch would land with a smack, but the sound it actually made was more like a squish. What was left of Tor's head was rocked to the side and I was spattered by flying blood flung off from his head. The eyeball on the left side of Tor's face popped from the socket and swung out at me hanging from connecting nerve tissue.

Now Morris West was back on his feet. He was coming at me too.

I backed up and threw another kick to Tor's balls and hit him with a left hook. I was hurting him about as much as if I had been pounding a heavy bag. His head and face was going to pieces, but he showed no reaction to anything I did to him.

Tor threw a wide, slow, arcing blow at me and actually hit the wall instead of me. I stepped backward and stepped on something, maybe a table leg. My foot shot out from underneath me and I went down to my knees.

Tor fell onto my back and grabbed me by the shoulders. Some kind of slimy oozing crud fell off of Tor's face onto the back of my neck and ran down into the back of my shirt.

I spun over to my back and kicked out with both feet and knocked Tor flying backward. Morris West was on me then. He fell on me and his knee found my crotch when he came down. I saw stars.

He clubbed a blow to my head and I punched back instinctively through a thickening fog.

Then I saw Morris West pulled up over me by hands that grabbed him by the back of his shirt and by the hair on the top of his head.

I saw through the fog that it was Johnny. He jerked Morris past him and threw him towards the turned over table in the kitchen. The top of Morris's head ripped loose in Johnny's hand. He looked at it and threw it away saying, "Damn, that's fuckin' sick."

Johnny pulled out a pump sawed off shotgun from underneath his coat and chambered a shell.

When Tor got to his feet, Johnny let rip with the shotgun and blew off both of his legs from below the knees.

I got to my feet and when Morris West did the same, Johnny blew his legs out from underneath him too.

The two were still trying to come after us like windup toys but without their legs they weren't coming too fast.

Johnny looked at them and said, "Christ, these are some dedicated uglies here."

"No doubt about that," I told him. "Hey, thanks for the help."

"About a minute after you left," he said. "I got to thinkin I better come help. I know you can't do shit without me."

"That's about the truth," I told him.

We kicked Tor Ambrose out of the way and checked the two bedrooms for Julia and Felicia.

They were gone.

Everything was torn up in the rooms and the furniture was busted up, but there wasn't any blood in the bedrooms.

"They must have been taken somewhere," I told Johnny. "And these two uglies were left here to take care of me."

"That's what it looks like," Johnny answered.

"I'm gonna have to find Julia and Felicia fast. Are you in this with me?"

Johnny gave me a strange look and said, "Motherfucker, I'm here ain't I. I just shot two zombie things for you and you ask me if I'm in this. Shit, I should shoot you for bein so fuckin stupid."

"I was just askin Bro," I said.

"Yeah, well you don't have to fuckin ask," he said.

CHAPTER 46
OLD FRIENDS

We were going to use Julia's phone to call Graham Nash but it had been ripped out of the wall. I figured that Graham, with his connections, might have some information about where Julia and Felicia might have been taken.

We went out through the front door and got into Johnny's car because what was left of Tor and Morris kept dragging themselves after us and we didn't want to have to keep kicking them off. We got in Johnny's car because his heater was a lot better than mine and I was tired of sticking my head out the window to see.

The snow was still coming down furiously but Johnny's defroster was handling it pretty good.

Johnny was behind the wheel and he asked me, "Where the hell do we go now?"

"Well, let's see," I said and looked back toward the house. I saw Tor drag himself out onto the porch, reaching toward the car each time he pulled himself forward. "Let's drive down the road," I told Johnny and he pulled out.

"All right," he said. "Where to?"

I thought for a few moments and said, "What do all these people who are involved in this have in common?"

"Fuck, I don't know," Johnny said. "You've been in the middle of this shit. You tell me."

"Well, Tor was the head of the Jamaican dealers and Morris worked for him," I told Johnny. "Graham told me that Robert Perry started importing drugs into this area after the Jamaicans were gone."

"So fuckin what," Johnny said. "There's been drugs in these neighborhoods since the stone age. It wouldn't surprise me if they found out the reason the Cahokia Indians vanished was because they smoked too much crack. They might of got so stoned that the whole Cahokia civilization might have forgot where the river was and marched their ass right in there and drowned."

"Well, I don't care who the drug lord around here was five hundred years ago," I told Johnny. "I just need to know who the new kid on the block is. Whoever is getting set to take over now, I'd bet that's who took Julia and Felicia."

"Why would they do that," Johnny said. "Julia and Felicia don't have shit to do with anything in the drug trade."

"No," I said. "But Julia and Felicia are just a tool to get to me. I'm the threat because of what I did to Tor's business."

"All right," Johnny said. "Who do we know that might know who this new dealer in town is?"

I thought for a moment and said, "We don't want to talk to someone who works for the new head of the drug trade either."

Johnny said, "Or if he does work for the new guy then he needs to be so far down in the chain of command that he could care less what happens to the big man."

"He'd probably be like one of these street junkies," I told Johnny. "Who sell just enough drugs to keep themselves stoned all the time."

"Who do we know like that?" Johnny asked.

I considered that for a moment and said, "Do you know where Marco Rios lives?"

"Yeah," Johnny said. He hit the gas and spun the wheels. The car did a donut on the icy road spinning completely around and stopped, heading back the way we had been coming from.

I grabbed the dash and yelled, "Damn, man!" as the world spun around me. When we were stopped I said, "Why the hell did you do that?"

"Cause we're in a hurry," Johnny said and drove toward downtown.

*   *   *

Johnny drove down Main Street then turned north on Franklin Avenue. Where the other streets had ruts in them from vehicles driving through the snow, on this street there were no ruts at all. Only a couple of sets of footprints marred the smooth top of the snow in the street.

Johnny stopped his car in the middle of the street at the entrance to Franklin Avenue.

"If I drive down there, I'll be stuck bigger than shit," he said. "It's only about a half block to where Marcos is staying anyway. We can walk from here."

We both got out of the car into knee deep snow. Johnny pointed to an office building that was boarded up and appeared dark and deserted. "Marcos stays in there," he said. "With a whole group of other crack heads."

Johnny left his car running and we went walking down the street. He carried his pump sawed off shotgun with him. I reloaded my Thirty-Eight and slid it back into my holster. The snow was slowing down a little bit, but the wind was still blowing with a bitter stinging force.

I followed Johnny to the east side of the street and onto the snow covered sidewalk. I walked right next to Johnny and he had to shout at me to be heard over the howling wind. "It pays to know where these guys stay," Johnny shouted to me. "If someone breaks into my place and steals something, I'm coming straight here. If anybody gets broken into around here, it's a sure bet that one of these guys had something to do with it."

Johnny led me down a stairway at the side of the building. There was a metal door that he pushed open and we stepped through it into the basement of the building.

We shut the door behind us and stood still for a minute so our eyes could adjust to the dim light that filtered in through cracks in the floor and small windows at ground level. The basement was divided into different rooms with a central hallway between all of them.

We heard voices and a rasping cough coming from one of the rooms ahead. A flickering light was coming from the third room. We walked toward the flickering light and knew that's where the voices and coughing was coming from.

The floor was a cold cement basement floor and we heard the wind howling through broken windows and cracks in walls. We breathed out steam in front of us as we walked toward the room where the voices and light was. It wasn't as cold in here as it was outside but it was nowhere near what you'd call warm.

Dust motes swirled around our heads as we walked along the grimy floor.

We went to the third room and through the doorway. There were six ragged looking men sitting or laying around a fire built in the center of the floor. They were laying or sitting on a ring of old soiled mattresses with tattered blankets wrapped around them.

They didn't even seem to notice us as they passed a crack pipe between them and took long deep sucking hits off of it. The blank, staring dead look in their eyes and the gray pallor of their Negro and Hispanic faces reminded me of the way that Tor and Morris looked when I'd first seen them in Julia's house this afternoon. The only difference I could see in these zombies and what Tor and Morris had become, was that these zombies would die easier.

I looked at the group around the fire and saw the man that I was looking for, Marco Rios. Marco had slid down a long way since I had seen him last.

When I'd first met Marco, he'd been a slick-dressing, fast-talking, arrogant guy, with a string of fine girlfriends and four fine, shiny, big cars. He made me a business proposition and I sold cocaine for him. We made a lot of money together, even if neither of us had anything to show for it now.

Marco started his downward slide when he started doing the drugs he was selling. At first Marco wouldn't touch anything stronger than a Budweiser. After a while though, I guess the stress got to him. Marco started smoking dope first.

He said it calmed his nerves.

This was about the same time I was hired to bring home Lisa Rios, his daughter, after she ran away. If I'd have known then what Marco was doing to his daughter, I never would have taken her home. He was fucking his own child.

Marco went downhill real quickly after Lisa turned eighteen and moved out. He started using his own cocaine heavily. He didn't keep track of his business. His dealers started stealing from him and his girlfriends deserted him when his money started getting tight. Then Marco got busted. He was down to selling his own stuff on the street when it happened. Marco actually walked up to an undercover cop in Wilson Park in Granite City and tried to sell him some crack.

The first rule you learn in the drug dealing business is never approach someone that you don't know to sell them drugs. Marco actually left his own city, East St. Louis, and went into a predominantly white area, Granite City, and tried to sell cocaine in a park where children were playing.

It was not a good idea.

Marco was sentenced to five years at Menard State Prison. I was surprised Marco didn't get twenty years considering where he was caught selling.

Marco got out of prison after thirteen months and tried to go right back to selling crack. Only the junkies were stupid enough to buy from him since he was known as a narc.

Marco took a long deep hit off the crack pipe. He handed the pipe to the guy next to him and started choking on the smoke that he was fighting to keep in his lungs.

We stepped out of the shadows and into the circle of light created by the fire. Marco saw me and let loose of his lung full of smoke. A cloud of gray smoke was expelled from Marco's mouth and his eyes rolled up into his head. He fell backward onto the mattress and started wheezing and coughing like an emphysema patient.

Johnny waved his shotgun around and the crack addicts backed away from us and we went to where Marco was looking like he was coughing his guts out. Marco wheezed and sputtered and choked for about five minutes. About the time I expected him to keel over and die, he held up his hand and sat up straight and looked at us with red rimmed eyes.

Marco smiled at me through rotted teeth. He could barely speak. His voice was raspy. Marco said, "Hey, it's John ahhhhh, whatever the hell your last name is, and his faithful nigger companion. How the hell are ya, my bud?"

"You're not my friend," I told Marco. "I came here to get information."

Johnny spoke up, "Next time you call me a nigger, motherfucker, I'm gonna put my foot so far up your ass you're gonna taste shoe leather."

"Oooh," Marco said. "I may even like it."

"Look fuckhead, this ain't no game," I told Marco. "What I need to know is who's the main supplier in this area."

"What if I don't want to tell you shit?" Marco said and smiled again through those rotten teeth. "You two aren't exactly acting real friendly to me you know." Marco slurred his words as he spoke. I knew that the crack had already had the desired effect on his brain.

This man was someone that I now had an intense hatred for. He once had been a good friend. When I heard what Marco had been doing to his daughter, it really drove me crazy that he used me to bring her home.

I pulled out my Thirty-Eight and pointed it at Marco Rios' forehead. "You're gonna tell me what I want to know," I told Marco. "Or I'm gonna blow your fucking brains out."

Marco looked past the gun into my eyes with a dull, disinterested expression. He had a weird look on his face almost like he couldn't remember where he was. "What's up with you man?" He said. "We used to be friends. Shit man, you do shit as bad as I do. Now you look at me like I'm a fuckin' bug."

"I never fucked my own daughter," I told Marco. "You're worse than a bug."

"Yeah," Marco said. "I wish you'd pull that fuckin' trigger. I know what I did. I messed up my own little girl. She wasn't worth nothing by the time I got through with her. Do me a favor man, for old time's sake. Pull that trigger. I still see Lisa's face all the time. Like she was when she was five and six years old. I even wonder sometimes what she would have been like if I hadn't of been her daddy. Shit man, I wanna fuckin die. So why don't you just fuckin get it over with."

CHAPTER 47
GIRLFRIENDS

I lowered my Thirty-Eight and knelt in front of Marco Rios. "This is how it stands," I told him. "We believe a little girl and her mother have been taken by the new supplier in this area. We don't even know who the guy is. We believe that he wants to get at me by using the girl and her mother. We got to stop him from hurting them. It's as plain as that."

Marco laughed. "You're still trying to be a hero John," he said. "Wish I could help you. Truth is, no one will sell me any quantities. So I don't know who the main man in East St. Louis is anymore."

Johnny spoke, "Who do you buy your crack from?"

"Now, if I tell you who I get my stuff from and it gets around that I told you, then I might lose my connection." Marco smiled as intensely as he could with his eyes unfocussed. "What's in it for me," he asked, "if I tell you?"

I holstered my Thirty-Eight. Standing up I pulled out of my pocket a one hundred dollar bill. Marco stood up and reached for the bill. I jerked it back out of his reach.

"This is what's in it for you," I told him. "Tell me who you buy from. You get the hundred."

Marco smiled at me and looked as deeply as he could with his glassy bloodshot unfocussed eyes. His face had a kind of indistinct sadness about it as though he was remembering something that he didn't want to.

"Shit man," Marco said. "I used to jerk you around with rolls of bills just like that one. Remember that?"

Johnny said, "That's how it is. What goes around comes around."

I held up the hundred and said, "You want the bill, tell me who you buy from."

"All right," Marco said. "I get my stuff from one of those chicks with dicks. I only know her by the name Candi Divine. That's the name she dances under."

"Where can we find her," I asked Marco.

"Usually I'd get with Candi at Roxie's," Marco said. "But the way it's snowing, I'd figure that the clubs are going to be closed tonight."

"Then where would she be?" Johnny asked.

"Candi shares an apartment with a few other half and half's," Marco said. "It's right next door to that gay bar, Faces. You know the place?"

"We know where it is," I told Marco.

When Marco reached for the hundred this time I let him have it.

We turned to walk away and Marco said, "Hey man, why don't you do me a favor and give me that bullet in the head you were promising to give me. I'm tired of this fuckin life."

I looked back at Marco and told him, "I don't think so. That would make it too easy for you. You're getting exactly what you deserve right now. The bullet would be the easy way out and I'm not gonna do that for you."

*   *   *

The ride over to the club, Faces, was going to take about a half hour in this kind of weather. I was glad Johnny had left the motor running in his car. It was warm in there. After the cold feeling I'd gotten all the way through me in the basement, I really did need to feel warmth of any kind.

Johnny drove toward where Faces was through the blowing snow. The club was a little way outside of town, so the streets hadn't been driven on much. Johnny drove slowly, right down the center of the two lane road we were taking, to make sure he didn't miss the edge of the road and end up in a ditch.

Johnny's old green Ford Maverick was doing a good job in this weather. For a light car it was gripping the icy road real well.

There'd been something I'd been meaning to ask Johnny since he'd taken care of Tor and Morris at Julia's house. We were a little ways from Faces so I said to Johnny, "You know Bro, when we were back at Julia's and Tor and Morris were coming at us like something out of a low budget horror film, you didn't even bat an eye at them. It was almost like you wasn't even surprised to see zombies in East St. Louis. So what's up Bro, why didn't any of this get to you at all?"

"Cause I'm a tough motherfucker," he said. "I can handle it."

"Come on, Johnny, "I said to him. "I'm as cold a fish as they come, but those two walking corpses made my skin crawl. How'd you know what to expect?"

"Well," Johnny said. "I'd be lying if I didn't tell you that Jeannette warned me about what Tor and Morris would look like. By the way, did you use on them what Jeanette gave you to use?"

"You mean that water," I asked. "In that little bottle?"

"Yeah," he answered.

"No, I forgot about it."

"Man you really are a fucking idiot," Johnny said.

"Hell, I was being attacked by the living dead," I told Johnny. "I didn't figure I had time to take an inventory of my pockets."

"Hey, John, just remember this," Johnny said. "When Jeanette tells you something about that magic voodoo shit, you better listen. She knows what she's talking about."

"How come you're changing your tune," I asked Johnny. "A while back, you told me you didn't believe in none of that stuff."

"Well, when I was a kid I spent the summer with Jeanette. Most of the weird shit that happened that summer I'd pretty much forgotten about," Johnny said. "That is, until you left my bar and Jeanette told me to help her make a shadow box for her."

"What's a shadow box?" I asked Johnny.

"That's what I'm gonna tell you if you'll shut the fuck up," Johnny said. "She had me fill up a big silver bowl with water. We set it in the middle of a table. Then Jeanette had me turn off all the lights. I tell you man before I even got back to the table I could see the water in the bowl giving off a weird glow. It was kind of a pinkish glow. I would of said, goddamn look at that shit, except Jeanette would of smacked me. So I didn't.

"When I got to the bowl and looked in, what I saw kind of freaked me out. I was looking in Julia's house the way it was when I showed up. The thing that was different was that you'd already lost the fight with Tor and Morris. They were both making a meal out of your head. Both of them was down on their knees biting chunks off your dome."

Hearing that gave me a weird feeling, almost like my scalp itched.

"That was when Jeanette told me that that was just one possible future. I told her I was coming out to help you and well, you know the rest."

"Well, I do appreciate you coming out and helping me," I told Johnny. "I was in kind of a tight spot when you showed up."

"No big deal," Johnny said. "We've been friends for a long time. You'd of done the same for me. Besides, who else am I gonna find that I can beat up on a chess board regularly."

"Not me," I told him.

"We'll see," he said.

*   *   *

We stopped in front of the club known as Faces and Johnny parked the car in the center of the road. He didn't pull up to the curb. If you parked at a curb with this kind of snow on the ground, you're probably going to be stuck there.

Faces was surprisingly still open. The place was like a small bar. There was a neon sign in the front window showing the outline of two theater masks and the name Faces underneath it.

"Let's go see your girlfriend," I told Johnny and popped my door open.

"You can kiss my black ass," Johnny said and we got out of the car into the cold storm.

The club was at the end of the street so there was only one house beside the club. We trudged through the snow to that house. It was a small house with yellow aluminum siding. A light shown in the front window through dirty white curtains.

Just before we got to the three steps in front of the run down house Johnny tapped me on the arm. "Hey man," he said. "I really do want you to stop that shit about messin' with me about Candi being my girlfriend."

"I'm just fuckin with you," I told Johnny. "You know that."

"Yeah," Johnny said. "But you've kind of worn that one out."

We went up the steps and I rapped on the door. There was music coming from inside that sounded like Johnny Cash. I think the song was Ring of Fire.

The door was pulled open and a tall skinny ugly looking she-male stuck its head out into the cold at us. I'd seen some scary sights before and never backed away. This time, I backed away. This guy, or girl or whatever the hell it was, had a pock marked face and a bush of bleach blond hair that looked more like a bleached out mop head than anything else.

This thing, with the worse makeup job imaginable, stuck its head out and pooched its ruby red lipsticked lips at me. The thing said, "Well, how can Alana help you?" It emphasized the words "help you," like a sexual invitation. The words of Johnny Cash drifted out the door, "Love is a burning thing, it makes a fire ring".

I looked at this creature and thought, the only thing that needs lit here, is your hair with some lighter fluid and a match.

What I said was, "We need to speak to Candi Divine, is she home?"

The thing looked at me with mock sadness in its eyes. "Candi is next door at Faces," the she-male said.

I started to turn and Alana reached out and suddenly grabbed my arm. "There's no need to rush off," it said. "You can come in and Alana can entertain you."

I looked down at Alana's hand on my arm then into Alana's eyes. "Take your hand off my arm," I said. "Or I will break your fuckin' fingers."

It removed its hand and I went down the steps with Johnny.

From behind us Alana sang, "Macho, macho man, I know how to please a macho man."

I gave Alana the finger from over my shoulder.

"Looks like you found a new girlfriend," Johnny said and laughed.

"And fuck you too," I told him.

CHAPTER 48
FACES

We walked to the club Faces and Johnny was snickering the whole way to the door.

As we reached the door I told Johnny, "You know all agreements about me not fucking with you about Candi being your girl are all off now."

"As long as you can handle me calling you Alana's bitch," Johnny said.

He opened the door and we stepped inside.

"That's kinda pushin' it bud," I told Johnny and he laughed.

The interior of Faces was dimly lit by beer signs behind the bar and a juke box in the corner. The music that was coming out of the juke box was some of that strange new wave stuff. It had a heavy beat and was played by instruments that I couldn't identify. The words of the song went something like - "In your little black book, you've got the names and the favorite persuasions of the people in the headlines. I'm in there under A, but I'm rated under B. You've got the photographs to prove it, but I swear to God it's not me."

I took a slow look around the club as my eyes adjusted to the interior of the building. My first thought was that the song on the juke box was a perfect theme song for this club.

There were four guys standing and leaning on the bar. Three of the guys were wearing the leather uniforms of bikers. Seeing that there were no motorcycles out front and considering the weather, I could see that their clothes were more Halloween costumes than anything else. The leather was entirely for show. All three had long straggly hair.

The other guy with them wore a three piece suit. He was small and balding. He reminded me a bit of Barney Fife with his horn-rimmed glasses. He looked like a bank manager who just got off work.

He turned his back to me and Johnny as soon as we came through the door. It was like he didn't want his face seen. I looked at him and thought he probably just dropped in for a quick dick sucking before he'd go home to his June Cleaver wife and Beaver and Wally kids.

There was a row of booths on the far wall. A couple of ordinary dressed guys sat in one of the booths holding hands. In one of the other booths I saw that fat dancer that had looked so scary at Roxie's. She was sitting alone.

We went up to the bar. The bartender might have been a straight guy for all I know. He wore one of those bartender suits with the little vest and his hair was immaculate and perfectly trimmed. He was so neat and clean and tidy that I instantly figured, he's got to be gay.

"Do you know where Candi Divine is at?" I asked him.

He smiled at me with teeth that were so bright they made a chill run down my back. "She's been sitting over there," he said and indicated the booth where the big scary dancer was sitting.

We walked over. Just like the night we saw this woman attempting to dance at Roxie's, she had her hair dyed a bright shade of red. Her hair was teased and brushed out so that it almost looked like she'd stuck her finger in a light socket.

"I remember you two," the woman said, excited as we approached her. "You're them two guys caused all that excitement outside Roxie's a couple months back."

She looked at Johnny. "Are you all right darlin," she asked. She had a faded southern accent. "Heard you got a little hurt that night."

"Everything's healed," Johnny said.

"Well, my name is Barbara," the big woman said and thrust her hand out at us.

We both took turns shaking her hand and I noticed how big and strong her hand was. But it was definitely not because she was a man in disguise. Her hand was too soft for that. No, Barbara was just a big girl with a lot of energy.

"Sit on down, boys," Barbara insisted. "And tell me what brought you out here. I can tell this ain't normally your type of club."

We both sat down on the other side of the table across from Barbara in the booth. I slid in first.

I now said to Barbara, "We really need to talk to Candi Divine. Where's she at?"

"Right here boys," a voice said from behind us and Candi ran her left hand through Johnny's hair. He jerked his head to the side and bumped his head into mine.

"Chill out," I told Johnny. "You know you love her."

"Fuck you," he told me.

Candi laughed and sat down next to Barbara. "I know you want me," Candi said. "But you don't have to say so in front of mixed company."

Candi grinned at Johnny and wiggled her breasts at him.

"Fucking great," Johnny said and looked away exasperated.

"You don't have to say nothing to me," Candi told Johnny. "I'll do things to you, you can't even imagine, and you don't even have to say nothing."

Even if Candi was a hermaphrodite, with the build she had, having muscles on top of muscles, I bet she could do some crazy sexual tricks.

"We are going to need some privacy," I told Candi. "What we need to ask you about is a little bit sensitive."

Candi smiled at the both of us. "All the people here are my friends," she said. "You can speak about anything you want to here. I've got nothing to hide."

"All right," Johnny said. "I'll come right out with it. We need to find out who the new main supplier is in this area. We know you sell and we know that a smart woman like you wouldn't deal with anyone but the main man."

Candi looked at me, "Did he just give me a compliment?" She asked.

"I believe he did," I answered.

"There is hope for him," Candi said.

"Maybe a little," I answered.

Candi batted her eyes at us and gave a small sad smile. "But," she said. "I can't tell you who the new main man in town is. He treats me and my other friends too good to let you mess with him. Besides, you don't want to know who this guy is. He'd fuck you up without even thinking twice about it."

"You say he treats you and your friends good?" I asked Candi. "Is one of your friends Robert Perry?"

I saw by her face expression that she knew Perry. It looked like she knew him real well. I dove straight on in.

"Robert Perry is dead," I told Candi. "We know that his death was ordered by the big supplier in this area. He was carved up like it was some kind of ritual killing. So, if you think you can trust this guy, you better think again. You could be next for any reason or maybe for no reason at all."

Candi's eyes teared up and she looked at Barbara whose eyes were also tearing up. She burst our crying and buried her head on Barbara's shoulder.

It was a strangely touching sightseeing this big muscle bound hermaphrodite crying on the shoulder of this huge red haired 'Baby Huey' of a woman. Candi tried to speak and couldn't through her sobs.

Barbara patted her on the back of the head, "Take your time darlin," she told her. Then to us she said, "We all liked Robert but Candi and Robert were really special friends. If you know what I mean."

After a few minutes Candi was able to pull herself together. She asked me, "Tell me how it happened."

Well, I wasn't about to tell Candi that I'd went down to Atlanta to kill Perry myself. I said, "I had a business deal I was going to do with Robert in Atlanta. I talked to him and he said he was nervous about the new man in East St. Louis. I was supposed to meet him in his hotel room to finish our business. That's where I found him. Who killed him was obvious."

Candi dried her eyes on the back of her hand and smeared her mascara down her face. The black streaks emphasized her grief.

"I knew something was going to happen like that," Candi said. "The man calls himself Cyphre. Who he really is, we don't know. But he showed up about a month ago. Told us he'd make it worth our trouble if we sold for him and didn't buy from nobody else. I've made real good money too, but Robert had to go his own way. He wanted to be mister big dealer man. I guess Cyphre found out."

"Where can we find Cyphre?" I asked Candi. "There is something else that he has to answer for besides Robert Perry."

She sniffed back her tears. "Cyphre is the spookiest motherfucker I've ever seen in my life," Candi said, "You really don't want to go find this guy."

Then Candi told us where she had been told that Cyphre lived. When I heard where it was, I knew I didn't want to go there. But I knew I would.

CHAPTER 49
BELOW THE STREETS

One of the ways to enter where this guy who calls himself Cyphre was staying was through doors in basements. This surprised me. Evidently there was an entire neighborhood that was below the streets of downtown East St. Louis.

The gist of what I got from Candi Divine, and it was backed up by Johnny, was that early in the 20th century the downtown area was flooding over and over again. Either all the businesses had to move to higher ground, which would have put them out of business, or the ground that the businesses were on had to be raised.

The city chose to raise the ground. So downtown East St. Louis was raised one level, roughly twenty feet. Below the streets of downtown East St. Louis were streets of closed down store fronts, turn of the century streetlights and other things that had been left down there when the people left.

Johnny told us that he'd went down there a couple times when he was a kid. One of his friends lived in an apartment building with a basement. They found a door in the basement that was nailed shut. Being young boys, they just had to pry it open. They went into the hidden city down there and went exploring. Their first trip was uneventful but their second visit was not.

Johnny and his friend came upon a campfire with five men hunched around it. They sneaked up to the fire to see what the five were doing. When they saw, both boys couldn't stop themselves from screaming.

The five men were roasting a human body.

The five who were around the fire chased Johnny and his friend back up to the basement. They didn't follow them as soon as they crossed the door to the upper world.

Johnny never went into the underground downtown again. He never wanted to. He had forgotten the place had even existed, until now.

I had never even heard of the underground downtown until now.

That's where we were going.

*   *   *

There was a basement below Johnny's bar. He only used the basement for storing things like old kegs and stuff like that. Johnny didn't go down there too much. Maybe that was because there was also a door in the east wall of the basement.

The door had been nailed shut since before Johnny had bought the bar. He saw no reason to pull the nails and open that door. He knew what was behind that door. He didn't want to open it.

When Johnny was driving through the snow back to his bar he said to me, "So the guy you were hired to kill was Candi's lover."

"That's the way it looks," I answered.

"And you'd have killed him too," Johnny said a little testy.

"That's what I was hired to do," I told him.

"You're an asshole," Johnny said with a finality that was hard to argue with.

"I do what I'm hired to do," I told Johnny. "If it makes any difference, I was hired because Perry blackmailed someone into committing suicide."

"It doesn't make much difference," Johnny said. "No one's totally inno-cent."

"Yeah," I said.

"You might think about changing your profession," Johnny said.

"I'll take that under consideration," I told Johnny, even though I knew I wouldn't.

*   *   *

We stepped out of the car at Johnny's and into the blowing snow. Nei-ther one of us was really dressed for this weather and we didn't have the time to go looking for the right clothes. The cold weather was already starting to wear on the two of us. Johnny was moving slower and I noticed that he stumbled over the curb stepping up to the sidewalk.

I was definitely feeling the effects of the cold too. My face felt like it was stinging and my feet were ice cold and getting colder every second. While walking into Johnny's I wondered to myself, just how long I could last out in this weather.

I thought about Julia and Felicia and I knew I would withstand the ice and cold that was eating into me as long as I had to. As long as there was a breath left in my body, I was going to use it to try and make sure Julia and Felicia were safe.

The realization of what Julia and Felicia meant to me hit me like bricks dropped out of the sky.

For Christ's sake, I thought, I had never even had my hand in Julia's pants and here I was professing that I would die for this woman and her daughter. I was shaking my head side to side in disbelief at my own screwed up brain when we walked through the doors to Johnny's place and stepped inside.

Johnny saw me shaking my head and looked at me kind of strange. "What the fuck's wrong with you," he said. "You look like you got the mange."

"You wouldn't understand," I told Johnny.

"You're right about that," Johnny said. "All you white guys are fucking insane."

And you are right about that, I thought.

As soon as we walked into his bar Johnny shouted, "Jeanette!"

There was no answer.

Johnny shouted her name again. When there was no reply he looked at me with an expression on his face that had the ghost of unspoken fear on it.

At a trot, Johnny went to the back of the bar. I heard him climb up the stairs.

I walked to where the chessboard was still set up on the table where we'd been playing earlier in the day. In the middle of the chessboard a sheet of paper was laying.

The sheet of paper was a note to me.

It read.

Mr. Dark

I do so enjoy playing with you.

Now I have two more toys

to play with.

You are invited to the party, Mr. Dark.

You, and your friend.

Don't be late.

At midnight I break my toys.

Come to me Mr. Dark.

Stop me, if you can.

The note was unsigned. Just like the one in Atlanta. I had no doubt they were both written by the same person.

I heard Johnny moving from room to room upstairs, shouting Jeanette's name. She would have had to be stone cold deaf not to have heard his shouts from downstairs, so there was no way in hell she was here.

Johnny came stomping down the stairs and ran over to where I was standing. Breathlessly he said, "Jeanette is gone."

I handed Johnny the note. "What do you make of this?" I asked him.

He read the note and then looked at me, "It doesn't sound like he's got Jeanette. He doesn't mention her at all."

"No, he doesn't," I agreed.

"Then where's Jeanette?" Johnny said. "This ain't the kind of weather you just go and take a stroll in."

"I don't know where she went," I told Johnny. "But I do know I do need to go and find Julia and Felicia. You can go and find Jeanette if you want to."

Johnny laughed at that, "What would I do, walk down the streets yelling Jeanette's name. Jeanette's been taking care of herself since before we both were born. I doubt if Jeanette needs my help now."

"You looked kind of worried when you came back down those stairs," I told Johnny.

"Yeah, well I just have to remember," Johnny said. "That Jeanette ain't no ordinary woman. She can take care of herself better than either one of us can."

CHAPTER 50
INTO THE DARK

Johnny got two big chrome flashlights from a shelf under the bar. He threw one of them to me. He went back under there and came out with a box of shotgun shells.

He filled up his pockets with the shells. Seeing him do that reminded me that I only had my five shot Thirty-Eight in my holster with no extra bullets at all.

"You got any Thirty-Eight shells back there?" I asked Johnny.

"Does this look like a firearm supply store?" Johnny asked. "I don't have every kind of ammunition made."

"Figured you might," I told Johnny.

He pulled out a small handgun from a drawer beside and below the cash register and tossed it to me.

The gun was a chrome plated Forty-Five. It looked a lot like the one that I'd bought in Atlanta, and then tossed away. The only thing different about this gun from the one I'd bought in Atlanta was that it was covered in a thick dust that came off in my hands when I caught it.

"Check and make sure it's loaded," Johnny said.

I popped the clip out of the pistol and saw that it was loaded. I turned the clip upside down and saw some rust fall out of it to the floor.

"Do you ever clean this thing?" I asked Johnny. "Hell, this thing might blow up in my hand if I try to fire it."

"Leave it here then," Johnny said. "If you run out of bullets you can always shake your dick at them. That should scare the hell out of them."

I slid the pistol into my belt.

We went down the stairs and into the basement. Johnny pulled a chain in the middle of the ceiling and a bare light bulb came on.

The basement was cluttered with all kinds of boxes, equipment, bar fixtures, and furniture. Everything had a coating of dust on it.

I slapped the back of a chair and dust flew up into the air. "Your maid's getting lazy," I told Johnny.

"Yeah," Johnny said. "I need to fire her. She don't cook none too good neither."

He went toward a wall and had to slide some bar stools and chairs out of the way. There was an old beat up coke machine against the wall.

The door was behind the machine. Johnny put his shoulder to the machine. I put my shoulder to the machine. We shoved it to the side easily.

The door that we now looked at was covered with dusty cobwebs. There were nails driven through the door into the walls around it.

A pry-bar was laying across one of the chairs we moved to get to the coke machine. Johnny went and got that and started pulling the nails out of the door with the claw end. After Johnny pulled about half the nails out, he handed the bar to me and I pulled out the rest.

Johnny tried to open the door and it wouldn't budge. He kicked the door and I kicked the door and the door still wouldn't move.

The door swung in toward us, so it was going to be hard to get any leverage on it. I went around the edges of the door with the pry-bar. Then I grasped the door knob and braced my foot on the wall to the side of the door. Johnny grabbed me by the shoulders and together we hauled backwards with all our strength.

The rusty hinges screamed in protest. The door moved toward us about a half inch and stopped dead. We hauled and pulled with everything we had. Then I had a brilliant idea.

I turned the knob.

The door came loose and we were flung backward and went flying over some of the bar chairs and landed in a pile on the cement floor.

When we got to our feet and looked into the doorway what we saw was pitch blackness before us. We saw the stairs recede away into the blackness. It was totally dark. Not even a glimmer of light shown.

I looked at Johnny and he looked at me.

Johnny said, "Are you sure you want to go down there?"

"I'm sure I don't want to," I told him.

Then we grabbed our flashlights and without another word we headed down the stairs.

The blackness was so complete that we had to shine our flashlights on the stairs below us just to see where we were stepping. Neither of us spoke as we went down the stairs until Johnny whispered, "Damn, I hate this fuckin shit."

"Don't tell me you're afraid of the dark," I whispered back to him.

"No, I'm not afraid of the dark," Johnny said. "I'm scared of the shit that can jump out of it and grab my ass."

Our voices seemed to be eaten up by the blackness around us, almost as if it were a living thing hungry to devour anything entering its domain, even the echo of our voices.

"I know what you mean," I told Johnny as I came off the last stair and stood on flat level concrete. "When I get the hell out of here, I'm probably going to use a night light for a long time."

All around us was the unrelenting blackness. Not a spark or a flicker of a light was anywhere to be seen. It was cold down here too. A musty breeze blew past us and up the stairs. The air around us smelled like stale dirt. The thought came to me that this place smelled like a crypt.

"For anybody to want to live down here," Johnny said. "He must be a fuckin vampire or something. This ain't exactly the kind of place you take your girlfriend to, to impress her."

"You got that right," I said back. "If this guy is just a vampire, hell, I'll be really relieved. I'm figurin he's a lot worse than that."

"Which way do you figure we should go now?" I asked Johnny.

"Well, Candi said that she heard that Cyphre was doing something to the old Rialto Hotel. I think that used to be on Main Street. Assuming that they renamed the streets above the same as the ones below. That would put Main Street one block to the north running east and west."

We shinned our flashlights around and what we saw was eerie and weird. This had once had been the main part of East St. Louis. Storefronts were here. The paint on the signs were still readable. The store windows were boarded up and the doors were nailed shut.

There were lamp posts on the corners. Trash was strewn about even on these streets. I guess some people hauled their trash down here rather than pay to take it to the dump. There were even a couple broken down things that once might have been old fruit carts.

In this darkness there was the complete setup for a thriving downtown area. It was only missing a couple things; the people and the sky.

CHAPTER 51
SHAPES

"I don't remember it being this dark when I came down here when I was a kid," Johnny whispered to me.

The thick atmosphere of the dusty darkness made us unconsciously want to whisper and be quiet. You got the feeling that you were walking through a giant's bedroom in the night. You sure as hell didn't want to wake that giant up either. The giant from *Jack In The Beanstalk* could smell the blood of an Englishman. Well, neither one of us was English, but I sure didn't want to run up on anything unexpectedly in the dark that wanted my blood.

We walked out into the center of the street and started north. We were shining our lights on the pavement in front of us to see where we were going so we wouldn't fall into a hole. There were quite a few large holes in the street. The holes were probably caused by the repeated flooding in the past century after these streets were abandoned.

We walked north on the street and didn't talk very much. Both of us were trying to listen for the sound of anyone in front of us.

The darkness was thick in front of us like oil. I was hoping there wasn't any bats down here that would swoop down and take a bite out of our heads. We shuffled down the middle of the street and could only vaguely make out the shapes of the storefronts on both sides of us. They were like phantom buildings where ghosts lived.

I half expected the doors of those phantom shops to burst open and vomit forth dozens of jibbering, yammering shapes with long fangs and claws to match. These things would fly at us trying to rip us apart.

I kept one hand on my Thirty-Eight in my holster. If they came, I'd be ready for them.

We moved on through the darkness. I had to force myself to move forward faster than I was comfortable going. But I knew that we had to get to where Julia and Felicia were real fast if we had any chance of getting them back alive.

Johnny edged up to me in the street. He whispered, "Has it occurred to you that this guy, Cyphre, might be setting up an ambush for us."

"Yeah," I answered. "The problem is we don't have any choice. If we don't go after Cyphre as fast as we can, then Julia and Felicia will die. I can't allow that to happen."

We moved on through the darkness, neither of us talking. From the vague outlines around us, I could see that vines had grown down from the surface above and hung like thick snakes down some of these storefronts.

Johnny grabbed me by the arm and halted me. "Hold on a second," he said. "Turn your flashlight off."

We both turned our flashlights off. Our eyes adjusted quickly to the complete darkness. Except that it wasn't completely dark anymore. Even without the flashlights I could see the grayish outlines of the shops at the corners ahead.

We stood silently and listened. Voices seemed to be coming faintly around the corner ahead of us. The voices were so faint we couldn't make out any words but it was obvious that we weren't just imagining the sounds.

I leaned close to Johnny and whispered, "It looks like it's almost show time."

"You got that right," Johnny said. "Let's just hope we ain't walking into some kind of horror show."

"I get the feelin we are," I told Johnny.

"So do I," he responded as we walked to the corner and peeked around the edge of the building.

About a block away to the west, the old gas street lamps were lit. My eyes weren't used to even that dim light, so it took be about a minute before I could see anything. When I could see, I couldn't tell very much about what was going on from the distance. All I could see was that there were people carrying things out of one storefront across the street and into another building that might have been the Rialto Hotel.

I whispered to Johnny, "To get up close to them we're going to have to use stealth tactics."

"Yeah, that's right," Johnny answered back. "We're gonna have to be sneaky as motherfuckers too."

I looked around the edge of the corner again and studied the situation. Since everything was being carried out of a storefront on the other side of the street and was being taken in to a place on the other side, I wanted to be over on that side of the street.

"We've got to get over there," I told Johnny and pointed across the street.

He nodded. We both looked out past the edge of the wall and as far as we could tell, no one was looking our way. We trotted as quickly as we could across the pavement and hid behind the edge of a building.

Looking out past the edge of the wall, I saw just how easy it would be for us to be spotted as we moved from doorway to doorway.

"We need to go around the back," I told Johnny.

He looked that way and said, "It's pitch black back there."

"So what's new?" I asked Johnny.

"Not a damn thing," he answered back.

We edged back away from the main street and just past where the building we were hiding behind ended, there was an alleyway. Out of curiosity I had shown my flashlight upward to take a look at the ceiling of this underground dead city.

What I saw was that even though there were cement columns that helped support the cement roof that was almost lost in the dusty haze, the majority of the support for the roof was supplied by the existing buildings that were down here. I could see beams and supports attached to the ceiling from the buildings. It did occur to me that the city council probably didn't allow very much to be built above ground that wasn't directly supported by a building below.

Looking down into the alley, it looked like we would be walking down into a tunnel darker than the pits of hell. There wasn't anything to do but go into it.

We edged our way down the dark alleyway shining our flashlights on the pavement in front of us. The pavement appeared to be like cobblestones. It was an uneven surface to walk on since the spaces between the bricks seems to have been washing away. There were wide cracks and spaces between the bricks.

Down into the dark pit we walked.

CHAPTER 52
INTO THE PIT

My heart was beating furiously in my chest as we went down the alley. There was something about walking forward into a pitch blackness expecting an ambush waiting for us that definitely put me on edge.

The stones were slick beneath my feet.

We were about halfway down the block when Johnny slipped on one of the cobblestones and bumped into me. He jumped to the side and said, "Damn!"

Even in the darkness I could feel Johnny's tenseness. I half expected his fist to fly out of the darkness at me.

"Do you get the feeling that somebody's watching us?" Johnny said and his voice tone was all about nervousness.

"Yeah, I do," I whispered back. "The thing is for them to see us they'd have to have a lot better eyes than I do, because I'm practically blind."

What I said must have been almost like a cue because a body flew out of the darkness and rammed into me. I was knocked sideways into Johnny and we both went down onto the slick hard stones.

"Goddammit," Johnny yelled and I found myself being kicked by unseen feet while I was trying to get up.

I punched upward on one of the legs kicking me and was lucky enough to get the inside of the leg and my punch connected with someone's balls. A strangled high pitched squeal was uttered and that kicker fell away. I threw punches in all directions at anything that seemed to be attacking me and somehow made it to my feet.

I could hear Johnny fighting and cursing somewhere off to the side but in the dark I couldn't tell quite what direction his voice was coming from. I didn't dare pull my gun and start firing. Johnny might be the first one I'd hit.

Anytime I heard a sound, be it breathing or a step or a muttered curse, I threw a punch or a kick in that direction. Mostly I was landing glancing blows or missing altogether. In this darkness I was fighting like a blind man because both of our flashlights were gone. The only good thing was that whoever was attacking us seemed to be as blind as we were.

I wasn't taking too many direct blows because I was fighting out of a deep crouching closed boxer's stance. With my hands up and my elbows tucked in and my chin down and my knees bent, I didn't give whoever was swinging at me too many open targets to blindly connect with.

We were in such darkness that one of my attackers actually walked right into my two up raised hands with his head. I grabbed him by the hair to make sure to wasn't Johnny. This was straight Caucasian hair so I knew it wasn't Johnny I had hold of.

I brought my knee up into his crotch then slammed his face down on the same knee and tossed him away. I had a moment of breathing space and shouted Johnny's name.

"They got me pinned to the fuckin' ground," he yelled.

"I'm coming for you," I shouted back and the crowd was on me again, fist and feet flying at me out of the darkness.

Again I went into my protected fighter's crouch. I tried to march forward throwing short hooks at whoever was in front of me like a blind version of Joe Frazier. There were too many of them. They drove me backward with the sheer force of their numbers.

Johnny's voice came out of the darkness to me. He shouted, "Get the fuck out of here!"

I could tell I wasn't being attacked from behind and it seemed like all of our attackers were between Johnny and me. Johnny's voice sounded desperate but I knew he was right. After I landed a good left hook on someone in the darkness and dropped him and then landed a right hook on someone that stumbled away from me, I shouted to Johnny, "I'll be back for you." I turned and ran.

I heard him yell from behind me, "Just fuckin' go!"

*　　*　　*

I hated leaving Johnny like that, but there was really no other choice. There was no way I was going to be able to get Johnny free in the darkness with that many guys on us and getting myself caught wasn't going to help us at all.

Down the alley I ran and I could hear the heavy footfalls of my pursuers behind me. I could now see a little bit in the dim light, so even though I'd gotten spun around in the fight, I was still going in the same direction that we started down the alley in.

I could see flashes of light between the buildings as I ran past them so I knew I was down where the streetlights were lit. Thinking that I really wanted to be out of this darkness and somewhere where I could see my attackers, I ducked down one of those narrow passages and ran toward the street.

The thunder of feet followed me between the two brick walls into the passageway that I'd ran into. The thought occurred to me immediately that this turn had been a bad mistake. While I might have been able to lose my attackers in the darkness, out in the light my only chance would be to outrun them.

I knew I was no track star.

The question as to whether I could outrun this pack was answered for me almost the same instant that it entered my brain.

In front of me I saw the silhouettes of several men stream into the passageway blocking my exit and coming toward me. Without thinking I pulled my Thirty-Eight and fired twice.

The boom in between the brick walls was nearly deafening. But not so much that I couldn't hear the two accompanying screams that came immediately after my two shots. I stopped cold because more bodies streamed into the passageway in front of me.

I fired twice behind me because they seemed to be closer than the ones in front. Again I heard two screams following my shots. But still they came on.

Now the silhouette of a face loomed in front of me out of the darkness. I pointed my pistol at it and pulled the trigger. I was showered by the wet spray of warm gore as the head in front of me exploded.

Then they were on me again. I could barely move in the narrow passageway and they attacked me from in front and behind. I tried to use my pistol as a club and it was sadly ineffective.

Fists and feet flew at me out of the darkness. This time, I had no choice but to accept the punishment. There was no room to maneuver at all. Blows rained down upon my head one after another.

Then one really hard punch caught me square on the chin. I was almost grateful for the greater darkness that dropped down over me. I slipped into unconsciousness.

PART III

CHILDREN
AND
DEADMEN

Who has not seen a child
Pull the wings
From a fly,
There is much Cruelty
In Innocence . . .

-    The Walker in Darkness

CHAPTER 53
SACRIFICES

Cold wind and snow blowing into my face was what brought me around. I opened my eyes slowly.

I was sitting on a bench with my hands tied behind me looking out into a dark snow blown night. That wasn't all that I saw.

There were torches burning in a wide circle around us. Julia was sitting on one side of me and Felicia was sitting on the other. We were on the dome of a large rounded hill. A tree was growing out of the side of the hill and its bare gnarled branches leaned over toward us like a knotted skeleton's hand reaching to take us down to hell.

Except for the torches, it was a black snowy stormy night out here. A group of men, I estimated at least thirty, were milling around in front of us.

Felicia was shivering in the cold beside me. She had a coat and jeans on, but it was still too cold to be sitting still out here no matter how you were dressed. I looked at Julia and she looked at me.

"Did they hurt you?" I asked her.

She smiled at me, a grim hard smile.

"No," she said. "They're saving us for something else. I think it would have been better off for us if they would of killed us right away."

I didn't like hearing Julia talk like that. Usually she is a solid rock hard woman. She must have seen something really bad to have taken all of her confidence away like this.

"We'll get out of this," I told her.

Then I looked at Felicia. Her face expression was a blank. She stared straight ahead like she wasn't seeing anything at all. She was in deep shock. I was hoping she'd be able to come out of it. After what she had been through just since I'd known her, I wasn't certain of that.

Looking around me at the hill we were on and looking at the tree, I realized where we were. We were on one of the Cahokia Burial Mounds.

These hills had steep sides and actually looked like huge upside down bowls. I had come up the hill that we were on myself many times when I was a teenager and slid down the side of it on inflated tire tubes in the snow. Tonight would be a good night for that.

But we weren't here for fun.

I looked at Felicia and told her, "I'll get you out of this."

She looked at me and there was recognition in her eyes. Then tears ran down her face and she leaned her head on my shoulder and sobbed.

The snow stung my face and I grinned at the crowd of men milling around in front of us. "You sorry sons of bitches," I yelled at them. "Let me loose and I'll kill every last one of you with my bare hands."

The crowd grew silent then. They stood stock still and the crowd parted to let someone come through.

Everyone stepped aside and made a walkway for the one who walked among them now. He came straight toward us.

This man who walked toward us looked more like a boy than anything else. He was around five feet four and thin as a rail. He wore an African style ceremonial robe like he was some kind of a medicine man. His head was clean shaven and his skin was smooth. He wore the face of a fourteen year old kid. But his eyes were old and they shone with an evil light that only the ancient and bitter can possess.

He walked toward us with an evil grin on his face.

To my surprise Johnny was walking with him. Johnny was a step behind and to the side of him. It was obvious that Johnny was no prisoner. He was not tied up and he was carrying his shotgun.

The two of them stopped in front of us and the boy looked at me intently.

"Mr. Dark," he said. "I am Cyphre. I am so happy you could see fit to join us tonight."

"Let me out of these ropes and I'll show you how happy I am to be here," I told Cyphre.

He laughed at that and Johnny did too.

I glared at Johnny. "You're a sorry sack of shit," I told him.

He grinned at that. "I play for the winning team now," Johnny said.

"We were friends for a lot of years," I told Johnny. "I guess that don't mean shit."

"We were never friends," Johnny said and stepped right in front of me. "The whites only want to use the blacks. I was only playin' the game. Well, now we have the power to use you."

I surged off the bench and stood up. Johnny stepped back and snapped out a quick straight right cross that sat me back down on the bench. It wasn't a hard punch. It was just quick. It surprised me that the punch wasn't that hard because we sparred a few times when we were teenagers and I knew that Johnny could punch like a mule kicks.

"You hit like a bitch," I told Johnny. "I guess you lost your balls somewhere in the dark."

He laughed at that and stepped back behind Cyphre.

"Yes," Cyphre said to me. "Mr. Davis now realizes that the dark skinned ones were the first men. We were meant to rule this world. I am going to open the gate tonight and bring the Loa through. They will inhabit the bodies of this world's rulers. The Loa will answer to me."

"You're out of your fucking mind," I told Cyphre. "You expect me to believe that you can put spirits into living people and run the world that way. You've been taking too much of your own drugs boy. That ain't gonna happen."

Cyphre grinned his ugly smile, "It does not matter what you believe," he said. "You have already seen it. The Loa was what I put into Tor and Morris's bodies to use as my servants. Felicia has a special soul. Giving her soul to Abbadon, the sovereign of the bottomless pit, will allow me to control thousands of Loa. The world will be mine."

Just one more small guy, I thought, with a Napoleon complex. The only difference was that he had us tied up and he was getting ready to cut our hearts out.

CHAPTER 54
CYPHRE

Cyphre looked at his watch and smiled. "Good," he said. "It is one half hour to midnight. Time to start our ceremony to open the gate. It is good that you woke when you did, Mr. Dark, or I would have to have cut your beating heart out of your chest while you slept. This way, I get to hear you scream when my blade slides into you."

"Keep listening dog shit," I told Cyphre. "You ain't gonna hear me scream. You ain't man enough to let me loose. You gotta have these mindless wonders of yours do your dirty work."

Cyphre laughed, "You are right, Mr. Dark. Of course I will not let you loose." He waved some of his other men in toward us. "Put them on the stakes," he commanded.

It took four of them to hold me. They dragged me over to the crest of the hill we were on and cut the rope that bound my wrists together. Then they forced me down to the ground where there were four stakes driven in.

While someone stood on each of my arms and legs, someone else tied my arms and legs to the stakes. I tried jerking my arms and legs loose as soon as I was let go of. The stakes were solidly driven into the frozen ground. They weren't going anywhere.

I looked around me as much as I could and saw that Julia and Felicia were tied to stakes the same way that I was. Things were not looking good for us.

Cyphre looked down at me. He had a large black bag hanging from his left hand by a rope. He reached into the bag and withdrew a knife with a long black blade.

"This is the soul taker," he said to me and held the blade up over his head. Lightning flashed in the sky directly over Cyphre and the sound of thunder roared from the heavens. It seemed almost like the sky was acknowledging Cyphre's powers.

No, things were not looking good for us at all.

Cyphre laid the bag on the ground and reached into it. He came out with a handful of white powder and threw it into my face.

"These are the ground up bones of warriors," he yelled up at the sky. "I give to you Abbadon the soul of another warrior tonight. This one can guard the gates of your kingdom in hell."

The crackle of lightning answered Cyphre.

He walked to Julia and flung some of the dust in her face.

"I give to you the soul of the mother. The symbol of what is good in this world. Take her to your bedchamber in hell."

Again the lightning answered him from the skies overhead.

"But first," he said and grabbed a handful of the white powder and poured it onto Felicia's face. "I give you the untouched soul of the innocent. The rarest of souls that glows golden, I give to you."

He raised the blade up with the point aimed downward and stood over Felicia.

I jerked at my ropes and nothing was coming loose.

Julia screamed and I yelled, "Stop you fucking bastard!"

Cyphre tenses to slam the blade straight down into Felicia's chest. From behind him I hear, "That's about enough, motherfucker."

It's Johnny and he has his shotgun pressed to the back of Cyphre's head.

Cyphre freezes, then slowly turns his head and looks past the two barrels of the shotgun and into Johnny's eyes. Over his shoulder he asks, "Would you throw away the chance to rule the earth with me? You would show loyalty to these two and a white man when you could stand with the most powerful Bokor on this world."

"All I see is a fuckhead who's gonna hurt a little girl," Johnny answered him. "I was never with you. I played you, Cyphre, and you were too stupid to know it. Answer me a question you stupid fuck," Johnny said. "What does a smart man do when he's held down with a knife to his throat and he is told, join us or die? I'll answer for you. He fucking lies."

Johnny laughed and winked at me. "Now I got the gun to your head," Johnny said to Cyphre. "You gonna be our buddy now?"

"You are making a mistake," Cyphre told Johnny.

"Yeah, right," Johnny said. "Now, you make your boys cut my friends loose or I'll blow your head off your shoulders."

I said to Johnny then, "Hey, Bro, sorry I called you a sack of shit."

"No problem," he answered. "I've called you worse and meant it."

Johnny poked Cyphre with the shotgun in the side of the head. "I told you to have them cut loose. Do it now!" He shouted at Cyphre.

Cyphre laughed and told Johnny, "You do not know what kind of power you are challenging today."

Johnny poked him with the barrel of the shotgun again and in a harsh tense voice he said, "Do it now or I pull this trigger."

Cyphre tensed and sang out, "Seera, Seera, come to my aid. Come to me."

The snow blew into my eyes stinging them. Lightning flashed through the skies overhead.

Cyphre continued singing, "Seera, Seera, I call you to my bidding, Seera, Seera."

The wind quit blowing into my face.

The snow stopped falling. The snowflakes literally stopped in midair. They are frozen where they are. Stopped, suspended in their downward flight.

"What the fuck is this?" I asked.

I looked at Julia and saw that her face was a mask of near insane fear. I looked at Felicia and saw that she had passed out. I was really grateful for that.

Cyphre laughed. "Seera controls time," he said to me. "He is a demon who does my bidding." He stepped to the side of Johnny, who was now frozen like the snowflakes in the air. He took Johnny's shotgun out of his hands and threw it to the ground. Johnny was unmoving like a statue.

Cyphre's men were looking at each other and murmuring in hushed tones. They all looked frightened. These weren't the most intellectual guys that I'd ever seen and their superstitious fears seemed to be running wild.

"Do not be alarmed," Cyphre shouted to them and raised his hands into the air to calm them. "I will protect you in this place. So long as you follow me, no harm will come to you."

The air tasted strangely metallic. It left a copper taste in my mouth. My breath did not steam up in front of my face as I breathed out. The cold wind that had been blowing in my face was gone. As a matter of fact, the cold that was stinging my face felt like it was gone now too. It isn't that it was warm. It just didn't feel cold anymore. It was like we were disconnected from the world around us.

I focused my eyes on a single snowflake and realized that it was moving. It was just moving downward extremely slow. So what was happening I realized, was that time hadn't stopped. Time had been slowed down to a huge degree, so that everything had appeared to have stopped.

Cyphre grinned at me. "This is a very small demonstration of the power that I have at my beck and call. You never stood a chance against me. You are only an ant compared to me. Not even an ant, you are a gnat buzzing around a bull's head, annoying but impotent."

"Fuck you," I told Cyphre. "You'll never know what it's like to be a real man. You have to have a chance of losing before you know what it's like to win. Guys like you never take any chances at all."

"The time for talking is done," Cyphre said with a dismissive hand gesture. "Your words mean nothing."

"You ain't shit," I said to him. "You depend on all these tricks. Without all these helpers you call on you're nothing. You can't play on an equal playing field. You're nothing. Nothing but a little boy playing a game."

Cyphre had been looking down at Felicia getting ready to shove his knife into her heart. He now turned his eyes to me and looked in my face. "Shut up," he shouted with wildness in his voice sounding like the child I had called him.

I must have hit a nerve somewhere, although I had no idea how I'd done it.

"Hey little boy, go home and suck on your momma's titty," I told him. "You ain't ready for any power at all. You wouldn't know what to do with it.

Go home and play with your toys, little boy. You're in the company of grownups now."

"Silence," Cyphre screamed at me. "I will take your soul first," he yelled at me. "No one talks to me like that. No one."

"It's a long time overdue," I told him. "Your daddy should've spanked you more. Then you wouldn't be such a spoiled brat."

Cyphre jumped to me and slashed at my chest with the black obsidian knife. He ripped my shirt and gashed open my chest.

Cyphre stood over me with the knife poised to be slammed down into my chest. I actually saw tears in his eyes. So, this was the voodoo superman that everyone was afraid of. Whatever magic skills and psychic powers Cyphre had, he was really just a small boy crying for the love and acceptance of dear old mom and pop.

CHAPTER 55
THE RESTLESS DEAD

Cyphre dropped to his knees beside me. "I can control the wind and the weather," he cried at me. "I can control the Earth and the Heavens." Tears ran down his face. "You will respect me!" He shouted.

"You need to grow up," I calmly told Cyphre my mind working furiously as to how I could use his own loss of control against him. "That shit don't impress me. You're just another kid with some magician's tricks you got out of your Captain Crunch box."

He screamed then and I figured my little game was over. He raised the obsidian black bladed knife over his head with both hands and yelled, "I'll kill you!"

Cyphre's expression changed from one of childish rage to one of bulging eyed surprise. He looked down at his thighs.

Skeleton arms had shot out of ground through the snow. The skeleton hands were gripping him by the thighs and the ground that he was on appeared soft and mushy. He looked like he was being drawn down into the Earth. Cyphre sank down to his ankles as the Earth beneath him turned to oozing mud. He was being pulled down.

Cyphre screamed, "No!" He dropped the knife.

I heard screams coming from Cyphre's men and saw that the same thing was happening to them. Bare boned arms were coming out of the ground and bare boned hands were grasping the ankles and legs and feet of Cyphre's men. The ground beneath them was churning and changing to a thick brown slime that was sucking them down. They were being dragged downward through the snow and sludge into the waiting dirt beneath.

The screams from Cyphre's men were blood curdling. They cried out and screamed and begged for mercy from Jesus and a dozen other gods. But no gods were going to come to their aid on this night.

I saw them being pulled underground. First they were dragged down kicking and screaming to their thighs. They struggled and beat at the skeleton hands that grabbed them, but only more arms came out of the sludge to help. The claw-like skeleton fingers ripped and clawed at Cyphre's men tearing their skin open in hundreds of places.

They screamed and they fought but they were dragged down beneath the Earth.

Cyphre was the last one to go. His face was a mask of unholy hellish fear. He reached his hand out toward me.

"Help me!" He screamed, his eyes bulging and blood running from his nose. He looked at me like a lost child begging to be taken home.

Well, I was tied to the stakes. I couldn't have helped him if I would have wanted to. The bottom line was that I wouldn't have helped him if I could have. Cyphre was trying to get power by calling up the spirits. I guess the spirits didn't want him to have power. They just wanted him.

Cyphre gave one last choking cry, then his mouth was filled with the thick sludge of the land of dead Indian warriors and he was pulled beneath the Earth.

When Cyphre was gone, all was silent for one long moment.

Julia looked at me and I looked at her. The pure fear was gone from her face, but she didn't look overly happy either. Her voice was shaky when she spoke. She asked, "What comes next?"

The snowflakes were still immobile in the sky and I saw that even the flames from the torches were unmoving. The flames were giving off the same glow but they were as stationary as light bulbs. The flames did not dance.

So we were still in this strange half world that Cyphre had put us in.

As an answer to Julia I jerked on the ropes that bound my arms. "I think I can work my way loose," I told Julia. "It might take a little while, but it don't appear to be that cold out here anymore."

Felicia appeared to be coming around and as I worked on pulling the rope on my right wrist back and forth to loosen the stake in the ground, Julia spoke to her. "The bad man's gone," Julia shouted to Felicia. "He won't be coming back."

I was working the rope back and forth and the stake was beginning to come loose when I saw a figure come up over the edge of the hill we were laying on.

The figure was robed completely in black and had a black hood pulled over its head. It was moving slowly toward us.

I pulled with all my strength on the rope on my right wrist trying to free my arm. I jerked furiously at the rope but the stake wouldn't let go.

The figure pulled a long gleaming silvery knife from beneath the robe. It walked to where Felicia was still tied. It stood over Felicia as she pulled at her own ropes and whimpered like a scared puppy.

It kneeled down beside Felicia.

"Leave her the fuck alone," I yelled at the hooded figure.

The figure turned to me. It reached up and pulled the hood back. It was Jeanette. I breathed a heavy sigh of relief.

"If you ever curse at me again," Jeanette told me. "I will slap you so hard your grandchildren will cry."

"Thank God it's you," I told her as she cut Felicia loose.

Jeanette cut us all loose. It felt good to be standing again. Then she went and looked at the still frozen Johnny.

"I think I like him better this way," she told us. "Sometimes my grandson talks too much and he gets on my nerves."

Julia asked Jeanette what happened that made the dead take vengeance upon Cyphre and his men.

"Spells of power have to be done perfectly, or the result can be the opposite of what you wish to happen," Jeanette explained. "Cyphre made some mistakes. This place is a holy place where noble warriors are buried. That was Cyphre's first mistake. You cannot force the good spirits to do evil. He woke them up, but I directed them to attack him and his people. Cyphre did not know I was involved so he took no precautions against me taking control of his conjuring. He was a natural Bokor. One who was born with the powers to control the forces and call up the dead. The rest of us have to learn how to do what he did from birth. He was very dangerous and had to be stopped."

CHAPTER 56
FALLING SNOW

Without a word Jeanette stepped away from us to the center of the hilltop and raised her arms to the sky. She chanted out some words that I did not understand. I had the feeling that the words were from some ancient language that was old when western civilization was young.

She stood there frozen like a statue, then we heard a clash of thunder and the tree to the side of the mound was struck by lightning and turned to splinters.

The ground rumbled like an earthquake was taking place. Then it stopped and all was silence except for the wind. The snow began falling again and I heard Johnny say, "Hey, what the fuck is going on here?"

He couldn't remember anything after he put the shotgun to Cyphre's head.

We walked and slid down the side of the mound to where Jeanette had parked Johnny's car. The cold actually felt good on my face. It was good to be back in the normal world where snow didn't just hang in the air in front of you.

Johnny drove us back to his place. On the way he told Jeanette that he didn't know that she had a license to drive.

"I don't," she answered him. "But that does not stop me from doing what I must do."

At Johnny's, Julia telephoned a friend to ask if she and Felicia could stay with them for a while until her house was fixed up. The friend told her to come on over.

Sushi was at Johnny's bar when we arrived and wanted an explanation as to what we were doing wandering around in the snowstorm. When Johnny told her an abbreviated version of what took place she said to him, "You must be fucking crazy if you think I'll believe that story."

Jeanette laughed at that and told her, "Do not worry yourself child, you are too stupid to be crazy."

AFTERWORD

I drove Julia and Felicia to their friend's house. I gave Felicia a hug and she went in. I stood on the porch with Julia.

I looked in Julia's eyes and suddenly I knew I didn't want to say good-bye without saying a lot more, but the words were sticking in my throat.

After I stood looking at her in silence like an idiot for what seemed like forever, I finally blurted out, "I don't want to lose you. When I thought something had happened to you and Felicia, I think I went a little bit insane. I want us to be together and I don't know if I can live any other way now."

She came into my arms then and I held her and kissed her and tears ran down my face.

"We'll give it a try," she whispered in my ear.

Then she pulled away from me and said, "I do need you to quit drinking though. If we can make this work."

"No problem," I told her.

*   *   *

The next day the snow plows had been out and I got up about two in the afternoon. The sun was shining through the window and it felt good on my face when I looked out.

A lot of the businesses around town were closed because the streets were still hard to get around on. After I drove around for a while, I found an open grocery store that sold roses.

I bought two bunches of roses and headed to the graveyard.

I went through the rusted gate and tramped through the snow to the graves of the people who I know. First I went to Lisa Rio's grave and I cleaned the snow off the headstone as good as I could.

Then I placed her bunch of roses on the snow over where Lisa is buried.

"Little girl," I told her. "These are for you. I hope you've found more peace in the next world than you did in this one. I know you deserved better than what you got."

I then turned to Kira's grave. I brushed off her headstone and placed her roses on the snow over where she lay. The roses looked like blood tears on clean white linen.

"Hello, Babe," I told her. "After what's happened the last couple days, I know you can hear me now. So if you're in the neighborhood, I just want to tell you how sorry I am. I should have been a better man for you. I can't change what's happened.

"I am going to let you know that I met someone and I'm going to try to be good for her. I hope you understand. I guess I wasn't very good at trying to kill myself. So I really do believe I should try to start living again."

As I was leaving I saw that someone was standing at the gate. As I got closer I realized it was Jeanette.

When I stood in front of her, she hugged me and whispered in my ear, "She heard you."

VISIT

SPEAKING VOLUMES ONLINE

HUGO, NEBULA, EDGAR,

SHAMUS, ANTHONY MACAVITY,

AGATHA, CARL SANDBERG,

ELLERY QUEEN, OWEN WISTER,

SPUR & BRAM STOKER

AWARD-WINNING

USA TODAY & NEW YORK TIMES

BEST-SELLING AUTHORS

www.speakingvolumes.us